F
Br   Brittain, Bill   c.1
         Professor Popkin's
         prodigious polish: a
         tale of Coven Tree

DATE DUE   DISCARD

Smith		SEP 17 1999	
	FEB 27 '94	MAY 7 2001	
APR 22 '91	NOV 25	MAY 1 4 2001	
Tan	DEC 4 '97		
FEB 2 '93	FEB 3		
Tan	FEB 24		
FEB 23 '02	NOV 3 1998		
	NOV 1 0 1998		
Tan	NOV 1 0 1998		
NOV 14 '02	NOV 1 7 1998		
OCT 25 '93	NOV 2 4 1998		
APR 28 '95	DEC 8 1998		

DISCARD

DEMCO

**Presented to
Mount Tamalpais
School Library
in honor of**

Joan Hofmann

by

David West
Christmas, 1990

Professor Popkin's
Prodigious Polish

Professor Popkin's Prodigious Polish

A Tale of Coven Tree

by Bill Brittain
drawings by Andrew Glass

HARPER & ROW, PUBLISHERS

For Robert Warren
—my editor, my friend—
who shares my delight with the people
and the village of Coven Tree

PROFESSOR POPKIN'S PRODIGIOUS POLISH:
A TALE OF COVEN TREE
Text copyright © 1990 by Bill Brittain
Illustrations copyright © 1990 by Andrew Glass
All rights reserved. No part of this book may be
used or reproduced in any manner whatsoever without
written permission except in the case of brief quotations
embodied in critical articles and reviews. Printed in
the United States of America. For information address
Harper & Row Junior Books, 10 East 53rd Street,
New York, NY 10022.
1 2 3 4 5 6 7 8 9 10
First Edition

Library of Congress Cataloging-in-Publication Data
Brittain, Bill.
  Professor Popkin's prodigious polish : a tale of Coven Tree / by
Bill Brittain ; drawings by Andrew Glass.
    p.   cm.
  Summary: When Luther Gilpin sells Professor Popkin's magical
furniture polish to the townspeople of Coven Tree, strange and
mysterious things start to happen.
  ISBN 0-06-020726-4. — ISBN 0-06-020727-2 (lib. bdg.)
  [1. Supernatural—Fiction.] I. Glass, Andrew, ill. II. Title.
PZ7.B78067Pr 1990   89-78221
[Fic]—dc20   CIP
                                                       AC

Chapters

CHAPTER ONE

Luther

Those of you who've heard my other tales of Coven Tree know there's more to our little village than meets the eye. To be sure, at first glance it appears to be just another tiny farming community, like dozens of others in this out-of-the-way part of New England. Still, those of us who live hereabouts can recall with shivers of terror those awful times when some—some "thing" was sent by the Evil One to walk among us in human guise, using our own hopes and desires and fears to cut a swath of chaos and destruction through our usually everyday lives.

Maybe it's because of the Coven Tree itself— the one our village is named for. We've all heard the tales of how, centuries ago, groups of witches called *covens* used to gather at that gnarled old oak down at the crossroads, weaving wicked spells and enchantments to plague mortal folks.

Or maybe the Coven Tree is only a sign, put there by Satan, to mark a place of easy entry into our world. There's just no way of telling.

One thing I *can* say. Before that business with Luther Gilpin and Professor Popkin's Prodigious Polish was over, every man, woman, and child in all of Coven Tree wished they lived somewhere a lot more peaceable. Or at least wished that Luther'd had enough sense to—

Oh my! There I go again, sounding like the Reverend Terwilliger giving a sermon in church. First off, we should get to know one another. Me, I'm called Stew Meat. Long ago I was christened Stewart Meade, but nobody's used that name in a coon's age. Running the Coven Tree General Store as I do, I hear all the local gossip. So if there's anything you'd like to know about our village, I'm the one to ask.

Now then, with the introduction over, let me tell you about Luther Gilpin. Luther's pa and ma, Simon and Hester Gilpin, have a middling-prosperous farm down there in the hollow on the way to Fletcher's bog. At the time my story begins Luther had just turned fifteen years old, and Bertram, his scamp of a brother, was only five. It was just after supper on an early evening in

July. Mr. and Mrs. Gilpin were in the living room, reading the weekly paper, and young Bertram was in the backyard, playing with some toy soldiers Luther'd fashioned for him from chunks of stovewood. Luther himself was sitting on the front steps, talking with Dorcas Taney.

"It ain't a man's job to be washing dishes," he grumbled, rubbing at his arms. "You should have done 'em up by yourself, Dorcas. That's what you get paid for."

Dorcas, the oldest of the Taney brood of children, often helped out at the Gilpins' place when keeping house got to be more than Hester could handle. The girl was paid her keep and a dollar a day, which her family sorely needed. She also got to see a lot of Luther, which seemed to pleasure her more than somewhat. Still, she wasn't going to let him get away with talk like that.

"Seems fair to me, Luther," she told him. "And wasn't I right there beside you, wiping the pots as fast as you scrubbed 'em?"

"But Pa and me was out in the fields all day, moving rocks with the stoneboat. By suppertime I'm dead tired."

"And I suppose you think keeping house is nothing but child's play," replied Dorcas with a little snort. "Let me tell you, Luther Gilpin, that helping your ma with sweeping and dusting and moving the furniture around and beating the rugs and getting the meals ready isn't exactly a restful day either. When there's work to be done, everybody ought to pitch in and help."

"Well, mebbe," said Luther doubtfully, scratching the back of one hand. "But washing dishes is one of my least favorite chores, and that's a fact. Ma's homemade soap is just too powerful strong for me. I rinsed three times at the pump out back, and I can still feel it prickling my skin like a swarm of ants."

"Best soap made in the whole state," said Dorcas. "There's not a speck of dirt can stand up to it. It cleans dishes and the laundry, and I even used it on the back step, where you dropped a gob of axle grease. It took up the spot like magic."

"Yeah, and if you use enough of it, it'll take the skin right off your body," Luther told her. "Sometimes—especially on bath night—I wish she'd buy some of those soap bars Stew Meat sells in his store. Maybe then I wouldn't end up looking—and feeling—like a boiled lobster.

"Soap-makin' day each spring is nothing but a lot of hard, stinking work, too. First off I have to haul out the barrel of wood ashes we've been saving up all year. Then there's lots of water to be fetched and poured through the ashes so's the lye will leach out. While I'm doin' all that, Ma collects the cans of grease that were rendered from the fat at pig-butchering time.

"Then I get a fire going out beyond the barn and heat the lye in a big kettle. When it's ready, Ma spoons in the grease. Oh, what a mess! The smoke stings my eyes something fierce, and the smell is enough to shame a skunk. Later, when the soap is poured out into flat pans and cools off, it looks like nothing but gray sludge. And powerful? I tell you, every time I use it, I feel like I've been sandpapered."

Dorcas wrapped her arms about her knees, drawing them close to her body. "Luther," she went on, "I've heard enough about your ma's soap. Talk to me about something else."

"About what, Dorcas?"

"Tell me how it's going to be when your folks get on in years, and you start running this farm on your own."

"It won't be just me. Bertram'll have a share of it, too."

"But he's younger. So it'd be up to you to make all the decisions."

"Yeah, I reckon. Only—"

"The way I see it, Luther, with just you and Bertram in charge of the farm, it'd need a woman's touch. You two boys don't know beans about cooking, and a woman could see you kept the house neat and clean, and help in the fields and all. I mean, your ma can't care for you forever."

"I hadn't thought much about that. Maybe I could hire some widow lady to come in and do for Bertram and me."

Dorcas felt a prickling in her cheeks, and she knew she was beginning to blush. She lowered her head so Luther wouldn't notice.

"There's another way," she murmured.

"Huh?"

"You . . . you could take a wife, Luther. I . . . I mean, the Heffinger sisters are looking to get married. And there's Nora Weeks or Letty Flaxer or . . . or maybe you've got somebody else in mind."

With every word she spoke, Dorcas's cheeks got redder and redder.

"Truth is, Dorcas," said Luther, "my plans don't include getting married. Or running this farm either, for that matter."

"Not running the farm? But your folks are expecting it. You've got to."

"No I don't. Oh, to be sure, Pa and Ma are able to make a living from the soil. But for me, I want more than just a living. I want to be really rich."

"And just how will you go about getting rich, Mr. Luther Gilpin?"

"A few months back Pa took a trip to Boston, where he heard tell of a man who traveled about New England selling fancy shoes. That man earned near five thousand dollars a year. Just from shoes! That's what I mean by rich."

"You . . . you want to be a traveling salesman? A drummer?"

"That's right, Dorcas. What could be grander? I'd make a lot of money, and I'd travel about and see what the world is like beyond the borders of Coven Tree."

And you'd see all those fancy city girls, too, thought Dorcas with a little sigh of sadness. "What would you sell, Luther? Shoes?"

"Nope. There's my problem. The man from Boston does that. I need to find something else that everybody'll want. And as soon as I do, I'll be off to where the bright lights shine all night."

With that, Dorcas sprang to her feet, sticking her nose high in the air. "Well, if living in Coven Tree isn't good enough for you, Luther Gilpin," she snapped, "then I don't see that we have any-thing more to say to one another. I'm going inside with your pa and ma. I expect their talk will be a lot more sensible than anything I've heard so far this evening."

Before Luther could reply, she marched up the steps and into the house, slamming the front door loudly behind her.

Luther looked after her, half hoping she'd return to say she was sorry for the outburst. When she didn't, he turned toward the setting sun, sinking down behind Old Baldy mountain.

"Girls!" he snorted angrily.

Twilight came and went, leaving Luther in a deep gloom. He just sat and stared into the dark-ness.

"Wait till I get done selling in a few years and return to Coven Tree carrying a carpetbag filled with money," he murmured. "Then Dorcas'll be sorry she ever spoke that way. But she'll be too late. I'll laugh at her and maybe throw her a coin or two, just so's she'll leave me in peace."

A breeze sprang up and moaned through the trees. Great branches rubbed together, and to Luther their groaning sounded like a soul in tor-ment.

The breeze got stronger until it was a steady wind. Luther looked off down the path that led to the dirt road.

What was that? Something was out there, among the tree trunks, hopping from one to another like a white rabbit.

Luther felt a shiver go up and down his spine. It was suddenly scary being outside in the darkness—scarier than he ever remembered it. The white thing in the woods seemed to be coming closer and closer.

Luther got to his feet, wanting to go inside to light and comfort and companionship. But before he could turn, the white thing sprang from the woods as if riding the wind and landed on his foot.

Luther grabbed at it to fling it away. Then he laughed as his fingers wrapped themselves around nothing but a sheet of paper.

Crumpling the paper into a ball, he threw it away. Strange. The moment he cast it back into the night, the wind began blowing from another quarter. The paper unwrapped itself from a ball into a flat sheet and plastered itself to his chest.

This time Luther looked at it. There was printing on one side. He took it up on the porch, where he could dimly make out the words by the light from the window.

SALESMEN WANTED!!!
Wealth   Travel   Excitement
These can all be *yours*

***

HOW?
The maker of
PROFESSOR POPKIN'S
PRODIGIOUS POLISH
is searching for
young, bright, ambitious salesmen.

***

The product you will be selling is a
Special Polish, made from Professor Popkin's Secret
Formula and GUARANTEED to give a glowing
shine and bring New Life to household objects. It
practically SELLS ITSELF. All our salesmen need
do is demonstrate the wonders of
PROFESSOR POPKIN'S
PRODIGIOUS POLISH,
and customers will want to BUY!

***

For each $1.00 bottle sold,
our salesmen receive a commission of eighty cents.
Within weeks, you can be RICH!

Luther could scarcely believe his eyes. Here he'd just been talking with Dorcas about being a salesman if he could just find something to sell. And now . . . this!

Then shivers ran up and down his back as he read the final lines on the page:

Luther made up his mind. He'd show that Dorcas Taney! Smoothing the paper against his leg, he folded it, tucked it into his pocket, and walked into the house.

Dorcas was seated on a little stool by the fireplace, mending a pair of Bertram's socks. At the sight of Luther, she stuck her nose in the air again and turned her head away from him.

Luther did his best to ignore her. "Ma," he said, "I need pen and paper. I mean to write me a letter."

"A letter?" said Hester Gilpin. "Who to, Luther?"

"Just . . . somebody," Luther replied.

Simon Gilpin looked up from the book he was reading. "In this family we don't keep secrets from one another," he announced sternly.

"It ain't exactly a secret, Pa. It's business. My business."

"Well, the pen and paper's in the kitchen," said Mrs. Gilpin. "But you take care and don't spill ink all over the floor, the way you did last time, Luther."

In the kitchen, Luther sat down at the table with the bottle of ink, the straight pen, and several sheets of foolscap paper. He began to write:

Dear Proffissior Plopkind,

It took him three tries, but he finally got the letter the way he wanted it, all done up in fine style, the way he'd learned in school. He wrote about how he'd always longed to be a salesman and practically begged the professor to give him a chance.

Finally he tucked the letter into a grimy envelope, addressed it, licked the seal, and pounded it flat with his fist. He'd be the best salesman who ever was. Look out, world! Here comes Luther Gilpin, champion seller of Professor Popkin's Prodigious Polish!

The following morning, Luther brought the letter down to my general store—where the Coven Tree Post Office is right behind the dry goods. "I'd be obliged, Stew Meat," he said, "if you'd put a stamp on that and mail it right off."

As he fished a coin from his pocket in payment, I glanced at the envelope. "Netherton, huh?" I said, kind of wrinkling up my brow. "I thought I knew every city and village in the whole state of Maine. But I never heard tell of that town. Where is it?"

"I dunno, Stew Meat," he replied. "But soon as the letter gets there, I'm in business."

It wasn't any of *my* business to ask Luther *his* business. I put the letter in the big canvas bag to await the noon train and listened to Luther whistling happily as he left the store.

It was about two weeks later when the big wooden crate with Luther Gilpin's name on it arrived at the train station. The wood slats of the crate were a dirty gray, and when the box was moved, a clinking sound could be heard from inside.

Oswald McAdoo, the stationmaster, sent word that Luther could pick up his goods whenever he'd a mind to, and the boy showed up right quick, clucking and chirruping at the big horse hitched to his pa's hay wagon. He signed for the crate, put it in the back of the wagon, and set off for home.

When he got there, Luther carried the heavy crate into the small toolroom at the rear of the barn. Rusty nails screeched as he levered off the topmost slats of the crate.

Inside, on a pile of wood shavings, was a letter. Luther tore it open at once.

Dear Mister Gilpin,

he read with a smile. He liked being called Mister.

You have been selected as our Coven Tree representative for Professor Popkin's Prodigious Polish. Your first duty is to demonstrate this fine product to as many people as possible. Just apply the polish with a rag and rub lightly. Once they see how ordinary articles gleam and take on new life, everyone will demand to buy!

The cost to the customer is $1.00 per bottle. Of this, you will retain eighty cents, remitting the other twenty cents to me at your earliest opportunity.

Good luck with your sales of
PROFESSOR POPKIN'S PRODIGIOUS POLISH!

At the bottom of the letter, scrawled in red ink, was the signature of Professor Popkin himself.

With trembling hands, Luther placed the letter on the workbench and turned again to the crate. He brushed aside the wood shavings. There they were—four rows, with six bottles in each row. Twenty-four bottles of Professor Popkin's Prodigious Polish!

Luther took one of the bottles out of its packing. The bottle was of heavy blue glass, with a cork stuck tightly in its top. On the label was a picture of a grinning man wearing a shiny top hat.

Luther went to the dusty window and held the bottle to the light. The liquid inside seemed almost clear, but there was a dark mass at the bottom as if the contents had settled. Luther tipped the bottle upside down.

Part of the dark mass came free of the bottom and began drifting through the liquid in eerie strands. To Luther the strands resembled bodies, caught underwater and screaming to be set free. He saw something else in the bottle that looked like a skull, with smoke coming from the eye sockets.

Somewhat frightened, Luther took his eyes from the liquid and glanced again at the label. There, just below the words

BRING NEW LIFE TO HOUSEHOLD OBJECTS

was the warning

SHAKE WELL BEFORE USING.

He shook the bottle. At once the contents turned a uniform dark color. It appeared to be blue, but Luther figured it must be taking on the color of the glass itself.

He pried out the cork with his pocketknife and picked up a fairly clean rag from the workbench. Holding the bottle in his hand like a fragile egg, he looked about for something to polish.

His eyes lit on an awl lying on the bench. Fashioned of the finest steel by Sven Hensen, the blacksmith, the awl resembled a great needle, nearly eight inches long, with a knobbed hickory handle at one end and a wickedly sharp point at the other. Pa used it often for punching holes in belts and harness straps.

Once, the awl had been bright and shiny. Now, however, it was blackened with use and covered with a thin layer of rust.

Luther dampened the rag with a small amount of polish. Then he lightly rubbed the rag over the surface of the awl.

The rust and stain disappeared as if by magic, and the metal gleamed like Ma's silver teapot after a brisk polishing with wood ashes. Even the hickory handle seemed to glow softly in the barn's dim light.

Luther could scarcely believe his eyes. He went outside, looking for something else to polish.

Pa was out in the fields, weeding. Ma and Dorcas were in the house. But in the backyard, Bertram was playing with the ten wooden soldiers Luther had made for him.

"Hi, Luther," Bertram cried out. "Pa came in for a drink of water, and he was asking for you. He wants your help in the fields whenever—"

"I'll go there directly," Luther told his brother. "But first I've got to find me something to try out my polish on."

"Look at my soldiers," Bertram said proudly. "All in a row, just waiting for the general to come and inspect them. Could you carve me a general sometime, Luther?"

"Sure, Bert," said Luther. "But first you've got to promise to quit tying my bootlaces in knots. When I get time, I'll fashion you the best gen—"

Then Luther stared at the row of soldiers as if he was seeing 'em for the first time. There they stood, brave in their blue painted uniforms. Each one had a twig-sword hanging from a belt of yellow paint. A large nail, which served as a rifle, was held stiffly across each right shoulder.

When Luther had first made the soldiers, they had looked bandbox new, like something from a toy store. Now they were dirty and scuffed, from Bertram's hundreds of pretend battles amid the dirt and pebbles of the backyard.

"If the Professor's polish can clean up those soldiers, it can do anything," muttered Luther to himself. He reached down and picked up the one at the end of the line.

"You be careful of him," said Bertram. "He's

the commander. See, I tied a piece of gold cord around his neck to show his rank."

Luther paid no attention. He dampened the rag with polish and swiped the cloth across the side of the battered toy.

Incredible! A single stroke, and the right half of the soldier appeared almost brand-new. Yes, there was still a scratch here and a dent there, but the paint itself was as fresh as if it had been brushed on only moments before. The nail-rifle lost its coating of rust and glittered in silvery splendor.

His hands shaking with excitement, Luther brushed the rag over the rest of the soldier. With each stroke, the grime of hours of play disappeared like fog under a hot sun.

He polished another soldier, and then another. Soon all ten were back in their line, fit now for the most rigorous inspection. Bertram clapped his hands in glee.

"All sparkly, Luther!" he cried.

If it worked this well, thought Luther, he'd sell those twenty-four bottles in a matter of hours!

Luther was already deciding how to spend the money he was going to make. Bertram was overjoyed by the appearance of his toys.

The two brothers stood in the backyard, looking down at what the polish had accomplished. Neither saw the stern glitter that had suddenly appeared in the painted eyes of the tiny figures, or noticed that the mouths were no longer smiling, but were grim slashes across their wooden faces.

Inspections, the faces seemed to say, were for cowards.

These soldiers were ready for battle!

CHAPTER TWO

Soldiers and Awl

Next morning, Luther Gilpin was a little late for breakfast. When he walked into the kitchen, it wasn't hard for his parents and Dorcas Taney to see why.

"Just look at you, now," said Dorcas through a mouthful of fried potatoes. "All dressed up in your Sunday suit, and your hair slicked down. That's a mighty fancy outfit to wear for working the farm."

"You're a regular popinjay, and that's a fact," Luther's ma added. "But those ain't working clothes, Luther."

"Oh, I'll be working, Ma," he told her.

"In those duds?"

"It's just that I won't be working here on the farm."

At that, Simon Gilpin threw his fork down onto the table. "Consarn it, Luther!" he exclaimed.

"Yesterday you took the morning off to go down to the railroad station. Now you want even more free time. When's it all going to end? There's many a rock out in the south field that needs two men to handle it."

"I only want two or three days, Pa," said Luther. "To do a . . . a special thing."

"Uh-huh," murmured his pa doubtfully. "An' just what is this special thing that's taking you away from your farm chores?"

"I . . . I'd just as soon not tell you right off," said Luther. "But if things go the way I'm expecting, we'll be the richest folks in all of Coven Tree. Then you'll be real proud of me."

For what seemed to Luther like an eternity, his pa and ma just stared at one another with strange looks in their eyes. Over at the sink, Dorcas Taney sighed deeply.

"I must say, I'm not too proud of you right this minute, Luther Gilpin," Pa told him. "Seems to me you ought to tell us what you're up to. Is it honest, this thing you're planning on doing?"

"Yes, Pa. I wouldn't act in a way that'd shame you."

Luther stared down at the floor. He didn't like the idea of keeping things from his parents. On the other hand, he longed to see if he really could sell Professor Popkin's Prodigious Polish before he said anything to anybody.

"Oh, let the lad have his days off, Simon," said Ma finally. "If he's got something special to do, let him work it out in his own way. Otherwise he'll be chafing around this farm for weeks, wondering what might have been."

"Well . . . perhaps you're right," said Pa doubtfully. "You take your two days, Luther. Three, at the most. But I'll be expecting you to work double hard, once your holidays are over."

"Thank you, Pa," said Luther gratefully. "I'm going to make you both proud of me. You wait and see."

"Just one more thing," said Pa.

"What's that?"

"I want Dorcas to go along with you. Sometimes I feel she's got more sense in her little finger, Luther, than you have in your whole head."

"Dorcas?" Luther cried out. "But I want what I'm doing to be a surprise. How can I do that if she—"

"Dorcas," said Ma to the girl, "you go along, just as Mr. Gilpin ordered. But you keep Luther's doings to yourself for the next few days, unless you believe he's up to something disgraceful. Is that understood?"

"Yes. Yes, ma'am!" Dorcas whipped off her apron. She could hardly believe her good fortune. Nothing to do for at least two days—maybe more—except be with Luther.

"Aww," moaned Luther. "Does she have to, Ma?"

"Either Dorcas goes with you," Ma told him, "or you stay home."

"Ohhh . . . all right. Dorcas, you go get yourself fixed up proper. I'll be waiting for you outside. Just remember, when we get to . . . to where we're going, stay out of my way. Hear?"

As Luther turned toward the door, Dorcas stuck her tongue out at him. Then she went to the kitchen mirror and began combing out her hair.

In the barn toolroom, Luther took from its crate the bottle of polish he'd already opened. "I'll bring just the one," he muttered to himself, "for demonstrating. No sense dragging the whole crate about. Then, when folks put in their orders, I'll make my deliveries."

He looked about the small room and found a cloth bag with a drawstring top that had once contained liniment for the horses. "The very thing," he said, slipping the bottle of polish inside.

When he came out of the barn, he saw Dorcas waiting for him on the front porch. Young Bertram was there too, seated on the rough planks and preparing to play with his wooden soldiers.

"What's in the bag, Luther?" Dorcas asked.

"A sample of my line of merchandise, dear girl," he told her. She scowled fiercely at him.

"I hate it when you get to soundin' all highfalutin' like that," she exclaimed. "Just tell me what you've got in there."

"You'll see, Dorcas. You'll see."

They walked down the front steps. "So long, Bert," Luther called back over his shoulder. "Have a good time with your soldiers."

Neither he nor Dorcas noticed the puzzled frown that was forming on Bertram's face.

Bertram grasped one tiny soldier in a pudgy fist, glared at it sternly, and shook the finger of his other hand in its painted face. "You will stand in a straight line," he ordered firmly. "You will!"

With that, the boy picked up each of the soldiers in turn and placed it so that the toes of the black boots just touched a crack between two porch planks. He continued his adjustments until the line of men was straight and true—the way soldiers should stand.

"That's better," said Bertram, getting to his feet. He looked down at his toys.

Strange. The toys seemed to be looking back up at him, and there was a touch of malice in each painted eye.

"And no sneaking out of place this time," he commanded. "Just stay like I put you!"

He turned away, covered his eyes with his hands, and counted to ten. Then he whirled about as if trying to catch his toys in some sinful act. Nine of the soldiers remained in file.

The Commander, however—the one with the bit of gold cord about its neck—had somehow left the line and now stood in front of the others, facing them.

"No! No! No!" Bertram screamed. "You can't move unless I say so! You're supposed to—"

Suddenly he caught his breath. It wasn't possible. And yet . . .

Had the Commander's head turned, ever so slightly, toward him?

He set the Commander back in its place at the end of the line. Again he turned away, and again he counted to ten. This time, when he glanced

back, the little wooden men were no longer in a line.

Nine toys were huddled about their commander, who seemed to be whispering to them, although Bertram couldn't hear a sound.

"I'll fix you!" the boy exclaimed. He scuttled into the house. He removed a length of string from the kitchen drawer where his mother stored oddments.

When he returned to the front porch, not a single soldier could be seen.

"Stop hiding on me," he whined. Never before had any of his toys acted so strangely. He looked about and saw four of the little men behind one of the supporting posts. With a flick of his hand he sent them rattling back to the middle of the porch.

Three more were pressed against the riser of the top step. Another pair was lurking amid the ivy plant on the windowsill.

The Commander had wrapped himself in a fold of the big pillow on the rocking chair.

Once all the soldiers had been gathered, Bertram laid them on their sides and stacked them into a pile, like ten bits of firewood. Then he wrapped the string about them, again and again, until they were all firmly bound together. He pulled the ends of the string tight and knotted them.

"There!" he said finally. "*Now* let's see you start moving around!"

He got to his feet, covered his eyes, and counted to ten. Then he looked down.

The soldiers were on their feet, grouped about the Commander. The string was lying in loose tangles on the porch floor. Bertram's knot was still in it. Somehow the string had broken or . . . But there was something else. All the soldiers had been carved in the same shape. Now, one of them no longer had its twig sword hanging from its belt. Instead, the tiny weapon was clutched firmly in a wooden hand.

Bertram began to feel fear grip at his belly. "Bad soldiers!" he whimpered. Quickly he reached out, plucked up a man in each hand, and squeezed them tightly.

"Ow!" he cried out in sudden pain. Hurling a soldier to the floor, Bertram squinted at the blood-stained palm of his left hand. The soldier's twig-sword had left a deep scratch.

Movement . . . in his *other* hand. He threw down that soldier, too. It banged loudly against the floor, and paint chipped off its jaunty cap. It lay on its back, staring up at the boy, and its painted eyes glittered with cold fury.

They're really alive! thought Bertram. But Ma and Pa would never believe such a thing. They'd just say he'd been scratched because of his own carelessness.

He grabbed the paper bag in which he kept the soldiers and, with a quick sweep of his forearm, pushed all the carved figures inside. Twisting the top closed, he plunged into the house and up the stairs.

Reaching his bedroom, he flung the bag into the darkest corner of his closet and slammed the door. Scrubbing away tears with a grubby fist, he went back down to the kitchen and held his injured hand under the icy water from the pump at the sink.

Above him, in the bedroom closet, all was silent.

No, not quite all.

From the paper bag in the dark corner came a gentle rustling sound.

Meanwhile, in the field just beyond the barn, Simon Gilpin was having his own problems. He had Phoebe, the horse, harnessed to the bull-tongue plow and was beginning to turn the earth in the vegetable garden. The long reins from the bit in Phoebe's mouth were looped behind his back, and he held tight to the plow's handles.

Suddenly he felt the reins fall to the ground. "Whoa, Phoebe," he ordered. "It won't do to have these things tripping me up. I'll just shorten 'em a bit."

He stepped out of the loop of leather and bent down to examine the buckle that held the reins together. The buckle's prong was already in the last hole in the strap.

Simon stood up again and searched his pockets for his Barlow knife. It wasn't there.

"I'll just go in the barn and fetch the awl to punch a new hole," he said, as if the horse could understand his every word. "An' while I'm there, I believe I'll put on my hat. The sun's hot enough to make one giddy, even this early in the morning." He mopped his sweaty forehead with a forearm.

"Stand easy, girl," he told Phoebe. "I'll be back directly."

Simon walked into the barn, grateful for its cooling shade. He snatched his straw hat from a nail in the wall and placed it on his head. "That'll be better," he said to himself. "Too much sun, and a man gets to seeing things."

He heard a rustling sound coming from the straw

on the barn floor. "Prob'ly a rat," Simon told himself. "Barn's full of 'em. The cats do the best they can, but . . . Well, let's see what we can do about this one."

He gripped a length of timber to use as a club and went over to the place where he'd heard the rustling. Gingerly he poked at the straw.

It was a rat, all right. But this one didn't try to run away, as most of them did. It was lying on its side and twitching. Blood flowed from a round wound in the side of its body.

"That's odd," said Simon. "It don't look like a cat's attacked it. More like it'd been shot or had some sort of a skewer stuck in it not long ago. But nobody's been out in the barn this morning."

He shook his head in wonderment. "It's dying, that's for sure." With a shrug, he clubbed the rat to kill it quickly and kicked the body outside where the cats would find it.

He entered the toolroom and glanced at the rack above the bench, expecting to see the awl hanging in its place.

It wasn't there.

"Somebody's been using my tools and not puttin' 'em back," Simon grumbled. "I wonder if it was Luther or Bert."

He heard another rustling sound. It seemed to

be coming from a pile of wood shavings in a corner of the room. Another rat, thought Simon. He walked over and kicked the shavings aside with one heavy boot.

There lay the missing awl. But the tool was not at all as Simon remembered seeing it last. Now, it was shiny and polished and appeared almost brand-new.

"Well, if one of the boys did cast you aside, at least he cared for you proper," Simon said. "You look store bought and just out of the box. And—"

Suddenly his eyes grew wide as he stared down at the awl. Had it twitched slightly as it lay there on the shavings?

"Naw, it can't be. Guess I just got more sun than was good for me." He leaned down and reached out a hand.

The awl leaped out of the shavings like a striking snake. Its sharp point glittered as it stabbed at the outstretched fingers. Quickly Simon jerked back, though not quite fast enough. He felt a stinging pain as the awl scratched the ball of his thumb.

"Oww!" Simon cried. He looked down at the awl, which was now lying on the earthen floor, several feet from its first position.

He shook his head hard, unable to believe what

his eyes were telling him. The awl quivered as if preparing for another strike.

Simon took a quick step backward. At the same time he sucked at his injured thumb, tasting blood in his mouth. The awl seemed to relax slightly. Its tip, however, remained pointing straight at Simon.

He inched his way first left, and then right. The point followed his every move as if turned by some unseen force.

"I must be getting the milligrubs or some other sickness," said Simon with a little moan. "It ain't real for a tool to be moving all by itself." Had it not been for his throbbing thumb, he'd have thought he was in the midst of a dream.

Then he saw that the awl, in its first thrust, had placed itself between him and the door of the toolroom. Dream or not, how was he going to get out of there?

He looked about. Behind him, on the floor beneath the bench, was a chunky log of hard maple. Simon had saved it with the thought of someday fashioning it into a hub for a wagon wheel.

Gingerly he reached about and grasped the log. When he turned back, the awl hadn't moved but was still pointed toward him menacingly.

With a quick jerk of his arms, Simon tossed

the log at the awl. Faster than sight could follow, the awl leaped up and buried its point inches deep in the dense wood.

At the same time, Simon jerked a heavy sledge-hammer from the rack above the bench. Then he stood astride the log, where the awl was struggling to release itself. He lifted the great hammer high and then brought it down onto the awl's handle.

WHACK

The point was driven deeper into the log.

WHACK

Most of the awl's shaft was now buried in the wood.

WHACK

With a final blow, Simon pounded the tool in as far as it would go. Only the wooden handle was now visible.

Simon gripped the handle. It seemed to throb and struggle beneath his fingers, trying to get free.

The wood, however, held it clenched tight.

"There! That ought to hold you!" cried Simon in triumph. "You can just stay there until you rust away!"

Then a new problem came to mind. How was he going to explain this incredible thing to his wife?

"She'd just say I'd been sipping at Avery Verser's applejack cider again," he told himself. "She'd never believe what really happened. I dunno as I believe it myself. So this is one adventure I don't plan to speak of to anybody—ever!"

As he was about to leave the toolroom, Simon caught sight of the crate his son had stored there. He looked inside. Then he took out one of the bottles and read the label.

"Professor Popkin's Prodigious Polish, huh?" he murmured. "Well, if Luther's takin' time off from the farm to sell this stuff, he's just wasting his time. There ain't nobody who'd be interested in this slop."

CHAPTER THREE

A Free, Personal Demonstration

At the first house Luther and Dorcas came to in Coven Tree, there was the sound of chopping from around in back. "Arvid Quist seems to be improving his woodpile," said Dorcas.

"Looks like as good a place as any to begin my career as a salesman," replied Luther. He walked around to the far side, where a short man with a billowing gray beard was splitting oak logs into stove lengths with an ax.

"Good morning, Mr. Quist," said Luther with an airy wave of his hand.

"G'morning, Luther . . . Dorcas," replied Arvid, sinking the ax into the chopping block and wiping his brow with a forearm. "My, ain't you all dressed up for a workaday morning. Is there something I can do for you?"

"No, but I hope to do something for *you*, Mr.

Quist. I have become the Coven Tree representative for a product so unusual and so effective that—"

"Now hold it right there, Luther Gilpin," said Arvid. "Am I right in believin' you're trying to sell me something? Because if so, I'm not—"

"I'm here to offer a free, personal demonstration only," Luther answered. "Then, if you find that you desire my product to enhance your lives, you can—"

"Demonstration, huh? It won't cost me anything?"

"No, sir. Not for the present."

"Very well—demonstrate."

Luther took the bottle of polish out of the sack and yanked a handkerchief from his pocket. He dampened the handkerchief, stepped to the chopping block, and gently wiped down the ax.

Arvid Quist blinked at the tool as if he couldn't believe his eyes. "If that don't beat all!" he said with a wide grin. "Ax must be fifty years old, but I bet it didn't look that good the day it was sold. Handle's shining like a new moon, and the blade appears made of pure silver. What is that stuff, Luther?"

"Professor Popkin's Prodigious Polish," said

Luther proudly. "Now if you'd like to buy a bottle, you can—"

"I dunno, Luther. Money's awful tight just now. Still, that polish did a jim-dandy job." Then Arvid's eyes narrowed shrewdly. "Say, now," he went on. "Why don't you go in the house and show Hazel what it can do? She's just in the kitchen there."

With a triumphant smile at Dorcas, Luther went to the back door. Through the screen he could see Mrs. Quist busily sweeping the kitchen floor.

Luther went inside. He took the broom from the astonished Mrs. Quist and wiped it down with the polish-soaked handkerchief.

Out in the yard, Dorcas heard Mrs. Quist's gasp of delight. "Why, I figured that ol' broom was ready for the rubbish pile. Now it looks brand-new."

"An' the polish'll work on the stove, too, Miz Quist. See?"

A moment later, Hazel popped out through the door, followed by Luther. "I never seen the like, Arvid," Mrs. Quist told her husband. "It's like we'd put a coat of blacking on that stove every day, instead of letting it get all rusty the way we did."

"So of course you'll want to buy a bottle of . . ." Luther began with a smile. Then the smile faded as he saw Arvid Quist shaking his head.

"The polish is a wonder, and that's a fact," Arvid said. "But Luther, we ain't got any money to spare. We do appreciate your shining up all these things the way you done. But buying? Not now. Maybe next year, when things ain't so tight."

Crestfallen, Luther put the bottle back in its sack and plodded out of the yard.

"Luther," said Dorcas, taking his arm, "that polish is amazing, and nothin' less. I never saw anything come as clean as that ax. And you didn't even have to rub hard."

"If it's so great," Luther grumbled, "why didn't the Quists buy a bottle? I was sure that once folks saw how well the polish works, they'd be standing in line to buy—even if it does cost a whole dollar."

"Even the best drummers don't make a sale every time," said Dorcas comfortingly. "You have to be patient. Let's go on to some other house."

"I don't feel like it. What happens if the next folks turn me down too?"

"Then you keep on trying until you succeed. That's what selling is all about, I reckon."

"But maybe I just haven't got the right words to say. Oh, Dorcas, I just hate it when people say no to me."

"Then perhaps you just ain't cut out to be a

salesman. So why not go back home and help your pa?"

"Nope. I'm going for a walk. I've got some deep thinking to do."

While Luther was pondering his future, Simon Gilpin was sitting in his kitchen, where Hester was tending to his injured thumb.

"How'd you get a gash like that?" she asked him.

Simon wasn't in the habit of telling lies. But at times, he could be awful stingy with the truth. He wasn't about to tell his wife how the awl had come alive out in the barn. If he did, she'd want to see the thing for herself.

He wasn't going to release the tool from the log where it was imprisoned, either.

Even now, it was hard for him to believe what his own eyes and his bleeding thumb told him was true. A thing made of iron and wood wasn't supposed to move about all by itself.

Still, this wasn't the first odd happening in Coven Tree. Simon thought back to the time when young Dan'l Pitt got to arguing with Old Magda the witch and paid a pretty price for his rashness. Then there'd been that feller Thaddeus Blinn, the wish-card drummer, and the evil Dr. Dredd, who'd come near to bringing the whole village to ruin.

Could something like that be starting in again? Simon felt a little shiver race up and down his spine.

"Here now," said Hester. "Let me scrub out the cut with some of my soap. That'll stop the infection from settin' in." After she'd washed the wound, she bound it with a piece of clean rag for a bandage.

"There now," she said finally. "That ought to do."

"Then I'd best get back to the garden," Simon told her. "Phoebe's out there, still hitched to the plow. She'll be wondering what happened to me."

"Well you be more careful with yourself, Simon Gilpin. I declare, there's something odd going on around here."

"Odd? What do you mean, odd?"

"First off, Luther's thinking he's too grand to be a mere farmer. So he goes off in his best clothes to do I-don't-know-what. At the same time, you injure your thumb. And even Bertram isn't acting the way he used to."

"Bert? What's wrong with Bert?"

"Just yesterday those wooden soldiers Luther carved for him were his favorite toy. But today he's moping around, saying he's got nothing to do. I asked him about the soldiers, and he said they was put away forever. I just don't understand the lad."

Simon rose and walked toward the back door. Then he paused. "Hester?"

"Yes, Simon?"

"You go to Stew Meat's store from time to time. Does he carry any kinds of . . . of polish there?"

"Of course. A whole shelf full. Why?"

"Did you ever see a blue bottle with the name Professor Popkin on it?"

Hester shook her head. "I don't recall any polish that looked like that," she told her husband. "Why?"

In his mind's eye, Simon could still see the crate of bottles in the toolroom. Could these have something to do with . . . ?

He opened his mouth to speak, but then thought better of it.

"Nothing," he mumbled. "I must have read about it somewhere is all. Now you put your mind at ease, Hester. Everything's going to be fine . . . just fine."

Luther and Dorcas didn't get back to the Gilpin house until nearly suppertime. But they could be heard arguing while they were still coming up the road.

"It seems like we've walked the length and breadth of the whole county," Dorcas complained. "My feet are so sore, I'll just die if I don't sit down right quick."

"I had some deep thinking to do," Luther replied. "Being a salesman isn't as easy as I thought it would be."

"But Luther, after the Quists, you didn't even try anyplace else. There's not a drummer in the world that can make a sale *every* time."

"But it was my first attempt. Oh, I'm discouraged, Dorcas. Mighty discouraged."

"You've got real fragile feelings if you'll give up after just the one try."

"That's easy for you to say. You wasn't the one Arvid Quist said no to."

"Easy? D'you call it easy, tromping after you all day and raising a bunch of blisters on both feet? It's beyond me what I ever saw in you in the first place. . . . I mean . . . Oh, forget that. It just kind of slipped out. Downright silly of me."

Supper was eaten in almost total silence. The only words spoken were "Pass the salt" and "I'll have some more potatoes" and such.

Hester Gilpin didn't want to seem like she was prying into what Luther'd been doing all day.

Luther wasn't about to admit he'd been a failure on his first try as a salesman.

Dorcas thought Luther was acting like a silly, stubborn mule.

Simon was still wondering if he'd gotten too much sun and had been seeing things in the toolroom that morning.

And little Bertram wouldn't say anything about the strange behavior of his toy soldiers. He was scared Ma'd dose him with sulphur and molasses and maybe fetch him down to Doc Rush's office.

When the meal was ended and cleaned up, the two elder Gilpins remained in the kitchen, going over the farm's account books. Dorcas knitted in the living room, while Bertram toyed with a ball of yarn at her feet. She noticed that the boy seemed to stay where the lamps were shining brightest.

Luther sat outside in the rocker on the porch, staring at the moon.

About eight o'clock, Dorcas took Bertram up to his room to tuck him into bed. The boy seemed oddly disturbed about something, and she hoped he wasn't about to be sick. After arranging his blankets, she hurriedly hung his clothes in the closet and pushed the door shut, anxious to get back to her knitting.

Neither she nor Bertram noticed that the door latch didn't quite click into place.

An hour or so later, Simon and Hester went up for their night's rest, and Dorcas entered her tiny room beneath the stairs.

Only Luther remained awake, sitting on the porch and licking the wounds of his failure as a salesman. Behind him, a lantern at the front window flickered dimly.

Suddenly Luther heard the clip-clop of a horse's hoofs and the creak and jingle of harness. Someone in a buggy was passing on the road. No—whoever it was, was coming right to the house.

Luther peered into the darkness.

He saw the horse first, its wide eyes flashing red in the light from the window. Then the buggy—a black two-seater, almost invisible in the darkness.

It came to a halt directly in front of the porch. There was a sound of boots on the path and then on the porch steps.

"I'm looking for a lad named Luther Gilpin." The man's voice was faint and whispery. "Would he be hereabouts?"

"I'm Luther Gilpin. But why would you be wanting me at this time of night, mister?"

The man strode into the light. "I've come to talk about your future, lad."

Luther scarcely heard the words. He was staring at the man's face. He'd seen that face before.

It was the one pictured on the label of every bottle of Professor Popkin's Prodigious Polish!

CHAPTER FOUR

Professor Popkin

The man grasped the brim of his top hat between two fingers, removed the hat from his head, and swept it in a wide arc as he bowed low before Luther. "Professor Mordecai Popkin, at your service, Mr. Gilpin," he announced with a wide, toothy smile.

"You . . . you're the one who sent me them bottles, ain't you?" Luther asked. He was more than a little frightened at having the professor show up in the dark of night, with nobody else about.

"The very same, lad. I thought you and I might have a bit of a talk. Rumor has it that you're becoming somewhat discouraged with the selling business."

"You're here to tell me I won't be allowed to sell your polish anymore, ain't you? I'm being fired because the Quists didn't buy a bottle."

Professor Popkin set his hat back on his head and spread his arms wide. "Perish the thought!" he exclaimed. "True, there is a certain—uh—request I must make of you. But you, Luther, have been appointed chief salesman for the Coven Tree area, and you'll not find me going back on a bargain we've struck. No, no, all systems are go, I assure you of that."

"All systems are . . . what?" asked Luther, puzzled.

"Are go," the professor repeated. "It's an expression used by the astronauts just before they rocket off into—" Suddenly he clapped a hand to his forehead.

"Dear me," he muttered to himself. "That won't take place for many years, will it? I become so forgetful sometimes."

Luther tried unsuccessfully to make some sense of the professor's mumblings. The only rockets he knew of were those shot off on the Fourth of July.

"You're downhearted by your lack of success this morning," the professor continued. "That's your problem, isn't it?"

"I sure am," said Luther. "I gave the Quists the best demonstration I could. I polished their ax, and their broom, and even their stove. But then, when I wanted 'em to buy a bottle of polish, they turned me down flat. Say, now—how did you hear about it so fast?"

"Oh, I . . . I have my ways," the professor replied with a vague wave of his hand. "And I wish to calm your anxieties and drive out your doubts about yourself. Come, Luther. Climb into my buggy. Let's take a ride while we talk."

"But it's night. It's pitch dark."

"Have no fear. My horse will find its way. I have no wish to wake those inside the house, but what I have to say won't wait until morning. We must seize the moment. Strike while the iron is hot, as it were. *Fortes fortuna juvat!*"

"Huh?"

" 'Fortune favors the brave.' It's an expression we used in ancient Rome when—"

"We?" Luther exclaimed.

"Did I say 'we'?" sputtered the professor with a nervous tug at his collar. "I meant 'they,' of course—the Romans. But come, lad, for time passes and time is money. Into the buggy with you, quickly."

As Luther sank back into the buggy's soft cushion, Professor Popkin chirruped to his horse and shook the reins. The horse wheeled smartly about, and they were off into the darkness. Listening to the clip-clop of hoofs on the dirt road, Luther couldn't figure out how the horse knew where it was going. He himself could scarcely see his hand in front of his face.

"The key to my selling technique," said the professor in a soft, whipped-cream voice that was almost a chant, "is demonstrating the product first. There's where your error lies, my boy. By now, I'd have expected that you'd have shown my polish to at least half of Coven Tree instead of just one family. Let everyone see its advantages, and it must follow as the night the day, as my frien . . . as Mr. Shakespeare wrote, that sales will occur. I confess, Luther, to sore disappointment that you didn't continue showing what the polish was capable of."

"But if showing it off works so well, how come the Quists didn't—"

"Did you expect, lad, that every demonstration would result in a sale?" asked Professor Popkin. "Nay, human nature being what it is, some are bound to refuse. My master—that is to say, my employer—knows that full well."

"You mean you have a boss too?" asked Luther.

"Yes indeed, my boy. The one for whom I work

is delighted when humans—that is to say, people—accept his offers of services. Yet he can grow furious when he is rebuffed, and often seeks to punish those who reject him. That's why he sent me here to . . ."

Suddenly the professor paused. He tugged nervously at his collar. "Sometimes my tongue gets ahead of my good sense," he murmured finally.

"That boss of yours doesn't sound very pleasant," said Luther.

"Enough about that!" snapped Professor Popkin. "Back to your problem, Luther. I tell you, you must continue with your demonstrating. Let enough people see what you have to offer, and you will ultimately be successful. I just hope we're not too late."

"Too late for what?" asked Luther.

"Uh . . . nothing, boy. Nothing. Now let me see. Perhaps the Quists will sleep late tomorrow. Yes, that's it. Early tomorrow morning, Luther, I expect you to be out, bottle and rags in hand, attending to the business of selling. By noon at the latest, you must shine up everything you set eyes on."

"I dunno. I figured tomorrow I'd help Pa move stones and just kind of get my nerve up before going back to—"

"No!" cried the professor, almost in alarm. "You must do the demonstrating at once!"

"But what's the hurry?"

For several minutes Professor Popkin was silent. As the buggy glided along the road, Luther noticed something most unusual. Although, in the inky darkness, he could see nothing of the professor's face or body, his eyes seemed to glow like two tiny lanterns. They floated in the blackness, never watching where the buggy was headed but constantly turned to stare at Luther.

"The night brings out a unique feature of my polish," the professor said at length. "Even as we speak, the darkness works its miracle on the Quists' ax and stove and broom. And I would not have this feature observed before your demonstrations are completed."

"I don't really understand what you're getting at," said Luther with a shake of his head. "But it must be after midnight already. If I get up early like you want, I'm gonna be so tired I won't—"

"You'll be refreshed, bright-eyed, and bushy-tailed," the professor assured him. "I'll take care of that. You have only to spread my polish hither and yon. Can you do it, Luther?"

"Mebbe. But my heart won't be in it. I mean,

after the way the Quists turned me down, just when I thought their dollar was as good as in my pocket . . ."

"Ah, then it's the money that's troubling you," said the professor. "That's easily remedied. If you had sold to the Quists and received their money, what would your share have been?"

"Eighty cents. But I didn't—"

"Hold out your hand."

Luther did as he was told. He heard the clink of coins and felt them tumble into his upturned palm.

"Eighty cents, Luther. Now do you think you can do as I ask?"

"I'll surely try, Professor. I just wish I knew what to say when I'm selling. Seems to me if I had some fancy words to use, it'd help a lot."

"Words mean nothing. Showing the product is the important thing. And it must be done early— before the Quists awake. Do . . . you . . . understand me?"

These last words were spoken in a low rumble, like the sound of distant thunder. To Luther they sounded almost threatening.

"Your polish really does work, and that's a fact," he said, hoping to get back on the professor's good side. "Soon as the crate got here, I tried it out on an awl in our toolshop and my brother's toy soldiers. Now the awl and the soldiers look almost as new as— Hey!"

Suddenly, unexpectedly, Professor Popkin yanked back on the reins, bringing horse and buggy to a jolting halt. Luther turned his head to see the two eyes glaring at him like a pair of fiery daggers.

"You did *what*?" the professor roared. "Are you telling me the awl and the soldiers have been coated with my polish for . . . for *two* nights now?"

"Well yes, but—"

The professor's shout of rage rang through the forest. Fright sprang up in Luther's heart like a living thing. Here he was, out in the middle of nowhere with what might be a madman. More than anything, he wished he was safe home in bed.

"You had no right to use the polish for your own purposes," snarled Professor Popkin. "However, what's done is done. Tomorrow morning, though, you must be both diligent and fast. Time is of the essence."

"I'm really sorry I got you riled up, sir," said Luther. "Mebbe we should just forget about—"

"No, lad. You're my agent, and we must both stick to the bargain we made. So that we'll remain friends, I'm going to allow you to keep the full dollar from all the polish you sell because of to-morrow's demonstrations. Fair enough?"

"I . . . I guess so," Luther replied. He couldn't help wondering why the professor was in such an all-fired hurry to get that polish spread around. But he was far too scared to ask.

"Fine, lad. Then allow me to return you to your home. Get a good night's sleep and be up early tomorrow."

While Luther was riding through the darkness in Professor Popkin's buggy, his young brother Bertram lay on his bed in that strange state halfway between sleep and wakefulness. Tossing and turning about, he'd succeeded in wrapping the sheets about himself until he seemed covered by a cotton cocoon. Now and then, little moans came from deep in his throat, and once he even cried out aloud.

There came a soft sound from the far corner of the room—from Bertram's closet. It was a dry rustling, like paper being crumpled and crinkled. This was followed by a number of clicks such as might be made by pieces of kindling wood being knocked together.

In Bertram's mind, the sounds became part of his odd dream, in which he was walking through a field made barren and lifeless by a recent battle. There were no trees, no plants, no grass—just parched, lifeless earth.

Slowly, silently on its oiled hinges, the door of the closet opened a tiny crack, not wide enough for a human or even a cat. But the clicking sound increased, and now it seemed to be in the bedroom itself.

Bertram uncoiled himself from the sheet and sat up in the bed, his mind still groggy with sleep. Could it have been just a branch of the tree outside, brushing against the windowpane, or . . .

On the table beside his bed was a stub of candle in its tin holder, and two sulphur matches. Ma had warned him never to play with the matches. They were for emergencies only.

Should he call Ma and Pa? No, they were too tired to be disturbed just because he was having a bad dream. He'd just roll back over and—

Click! Click . . . click . . . click

Bertram groped for the matches, found one, and scratched it against the underside of the table.

He lit the candle. The dim flame made eerie shadows all about the little room. Outside, he could hear an owl hooting in the darkness.

Raising the candle, he looked about. Everything seemed just as it had been when he'd gone to bed. There, the pitcher and washbasin, along with a small pan of Ma's all-powerful soap, ready for his morning scrub. There, his clothes, hanging from the nails Pa'd driven into the wall for just that purpose. There, the closet door, closed tightly and—

No! The closet door wasn't closed. A small crack, black as pitch, along one edge told Bertram it was ajar.

Click

Bertram lifted the candle higher. Then suddenly his eyes grew wide.

In the opening stood a tiny figure, perhaps six inches tall.

It was the Commander. The soft light glinted from the gold cord tied about its neck. But how, Bertram wondered, had the toy soldier escaped from the sack? How could it have made its way outside the closet?

Why did it appear to be gazing at him with such a hostile look in its eye?

What happened next made Bertram's mouth go dry as dust and his heart pound wildly within him.

The figure's right arm moved across its body, jerking the twig sword from its belt.

But a wooden soldier shouldn't be able to move. Besides, the sword had been glued into place. Bertram had watched while Luther did it. And the belt itself was nothing but a painted stripe on the wooden body. Then how . . .

Brandishing the sword, the Commander turned its head and called out something toward one of the room's dark corners. The reedy voice sounded like the chirping of a cricket.

Click   click   clickclickclick

Shifting the candle to light up the corner the Commander was facing, Bertram was just in time to see a single wooden soldier scamper across the plank flooring and scuttle under his bed. The nail-rifle was no longer resting on its shoulder. It was now held tightly in both hands, ready for battle.

Clickclickclickclick

From the sound of it, all the soldiers were huddled beneath the bed, preparing to attack. Terrified and not knowing what to do, Bertram swung about so that his legs, bare and white beneath the nightshirt that came only to his knees, hung down from the edge of the mattress.

Clickclickclick

The boy pushed himself out of bed. His bare feet touched the wooden floor. He prepared to bend down and—

Pop

The sound might have been that of a root beer bottle being opened. At the same time, Bertram felt a stinging in his right ankle, as if he'd brushed against a nettle.

He'd been shot! Nothing to worry about, of course. The bullet hadn't even drawn blood, and already the mild itching was going away.

Only how could his toys shoot guns made of nails?

Pop   Pop   Poppop

More firing. A rash of wee red spots now covered Bertram's ankle. Wildly he looked about. On top of the bed, the sheet jerked about as if being yanked at by something on the other side.

The soldiers were trying to climb up onto the bed.

Setting the candle aside, Bertram grasped the sheet in both hands and flipped it as hard as he could. Two soldiers were shaken loose and smashed against the wall. Wrapping the sheet about his arm, Bertram bent down and swept the area beneath the bed.

Clickclickclickclick

He counted seven soldiers tangled among the sheet's folds. They slashed at the cloth with their twig swords while Bertram gathered up the two who'd been trying to climb onto the mattress. Wrapping up the nine toys tightly, he tucked the balled sheet under his arm. Then, taking great gulps of air, he peered about the room.

Nine toys were his captives. But where was the Commander?

Taking up the candle again in his free hand, Bertram bent and looked all about the floor. Nothing. Yet the room door was closed, and the Commander was too small to have opened it. Then where . . . Suddenly Bertram knew.

He opened the closet door and thrust in the candle. With a smile of triumph he saw the Commander, cowering in a far corner. But if he tried to cover the toy with the sheet, some of the other soldiers might escape.

Bertram jerked his foot, and his toes struck the Commander in its side. The chunk of wood went tumbling into the paper sack from which it had escaped. Before it could recover, Bertram crunched the sack closed.

For a moment the boy wondered what to do next. Then he had an idea. Opening the door of his room, he stepped into the hallway. The battle, though fierce, had been quiet, and nobody else had been awakened. Pa was snoring softly, and Ma mumbled something in her sleep.

Bertram tiptoed downstairs, past Dorcas's room, and into the kitchen. With an elbow he managed to pry open the lid of the stove's firebox. Sure enough, a few glowing embers from the day's cooking remained.

First he tossed in the Commander—bag and all. He watched as the brown paper blackened and then suddenly burst into flame. Then he took the sheet in both hands and squeezed the toy men down into one corner. One by one he pressed the soldiers out and tossed them into the flames before they could fire their nail-rifles.

Finally he slammed the lid, listening to the roar of the flames as the dry, painted figures were consumed.

Behind him, the front door was suddenly thrown open, and then a kerosene lamp was lit. There in the living room stood Luther.

"Hi, Bert," he said. "What are you up to, this time of night?"

Bertram opened his mouth to reply. He couldn't think of a single word to say that'd possibly make any sense. Luther wouldn't believe him, that was sure. And as for Ma and Pa, they'd whupped him more'n once for telling fibs. It was all so impossible. The boy couldn't help wondering if even now he was really upstairs in bed, dreaming all this.

"What's the matter, Bert? Has the cat got your tongue? Why are you down here in the kitchen?"

"Uh . . . no reason, Luther. I couldn't sleep, that's all. But how about you? Where have you been, anyway? What would Pa and Ma say if they knew you didn't come in till all hours?"

Well, Luther wasn't about to tell anybody how he'd traveled about the countryside with Professor Mordecai Popkin and had promised to be up in the morning at first light to show off how the polish worked.

"I was just outside, doing some thinking, Bert. Tell you what. If you don't say nothing about my coming in late, I won't tell how you was up after midnight. Agreed?"

Bertram leaned down and scratched at his itching ankle as he thought this over.

"Agreed, Luther," he said finally.

With that, both brothers went to bed. All night they tossed and turned, for each carried a secret that made sound sleep impossible.

CHAPTER FIVE

All Over Town

Luther got up the next morning before anyone else was about. He found it hard to believe all that had happened to him the previous night. But in his mind he could still see Professor Popkin's eyes, floating in the darkness, and hear that voice, like the crackle of logs in a fire, commanding him to demonstrate the polish throughout Coven Tree. It had to be done early, too. Luther couldn't help wondering what was the big hurry.

"You'll not see me again," the professor had said at the end of the ride. "But I'm depending on you to carry out my wishes."

And what had Bertram been doing up so late? Burning something in the stove, that was sure. Luther'd smelled smoke in the kitchen. Why couldn't Bert have waited until morning, when Ma lit the stove to make breakfast?

These were strange times at the Gilpin house, that was for sure.

Luther put on his best clothes and prepared a cold breakfast. Just as he was finishing the last of it—and going over in his mind all the things he'd be telling folks about Professor Popkin's Prodigious Polish—Ma and Dorcas Taney came into the kitchen, rubbing sleep out of their eyes.

"Looks like you'll be taking another day off from your farm work," said Ma with a look at his white shirt and fancy tie.

"Yes, Ma. I got a big morning ahead of me."

"That's as may be," she told him. "But you'll have it without Dorcas. I'll be needing her to help with the laundry."

"I'd rather do my work by myself anyway."

On hearing that, the girl made an awful face at Luther, behind his back.

"Good. Dorcas, soon as you've eaten and got dressed, I want you to go through that big pile of wash. Put some of my lye soap on anything that seems extra dirty or greasy. It'll make 'em come real clean when we put 'em in the kettle."

"Yes, Miz Gilpin. I'll scrub real hard."

"Hmmph!" Ma snorted. "You won't have to do much scrubbing. I've yet to see anything a little

dab of my homemade soap won't make clean. Clothes . . . woodwork . . . people . . . it works on anything."

Luther got up from the table. Just as he was preparing to leave, his ma spoke up again.

"Luther, did you hear anything odd in Bertram's room last night?"

The question disturbed Luther. If Ma got to wondering about Bertram, she might also start asking where *he'd* been for all hours. "Odd?" he asked.

"Yes. For half an hour or so, I could have sworn I heard him bumpin' around in there and clicking little bits of wood together. I guess maybe I was just dreaming."

"I expect so, Ma." Before she could go on, Luther darted out the back door and headed for the barn to collect his rags and his bottle of polish.

He'd make himself a bushel of money. Then, no more farming and working from dawn till dusk. He'd be rolling in wealth, and all because of Professor Popkin's Prodigious Polish.

Say now, do you remember me—Stew Meat? I'm the one who's telling this story, and right here's where I come back into it.

Truth to tell, I'd been mighty curious about that

letter Luther Gilpin had sent to Professor Popkin. A couple of days before, when the train arrived at the Coven Tree depot, I'd asked a few questions of the man in the mail car. I'd also looked up some things in one of the books I keep on my desk.

So when I was unlocking the store just before eight o'clock and saw Luther Gilpin sauntering along the road out front with his bottle of polish in hand, I decided to tell him the results of my research.

"Come up here on the porch, Luther," I called. "There's something you ought to know."

He did as I asked. "Can't waste much time this morning, Stew Meat," he told me. "I'll be mighty busy, demonstrating the polish."

"Uh-huh. But about your letter—that one to Professor Popkin . . ."

Luther looked at me suspiciously. "You didn't read my mail, did you?"

"Nope. But I couldn't help seein' the address on the envelope. 1313 Gehenna Street, Netherton, Maine. Odd . . . mighty odd."

"What's odd about it, Stew Meat?"

"Well, you'll recall my sayin' I never heard tell of a city or a village in all of Maine called Netherton. Neither has the man on the mail train."

"What does that prove? Mebbe it's a brand-new town."

"So new the mailman doesn't know about it? Not likely. And another thing. That street — Gehenna."

"It's just a name, that's all."

"Are you sure? According to what I read, 'Gehenna' means 'a place of misery.' Now who'd go and name a street something like that? Finally, there's the number — 1313. Sounds like double bad luck to me."

"You sure are making a lot out of a little-bitty address, Stew Meat."

"Luther Gilpin, you know as well as I do that Coven Tree isn't like other villages. Satan himself seems to have picked out this place to try all kinds of mischief. The last thing we need around here is more problems of that kind. So I'd warn you to be real careful about the results of a letter that . . ."

Luther was only half listening. In imagination, he saw himself as a wealthy businessman, living in a grand house with servants to wait on his every need and a fine carriage to ride about in.

"I don't mean to be rude, Stew Meat," he said, "but you're gettin' mighty het up over just a little ol' letter."

"It stands to reason that if there was no town to deliver your mail to, it ended up in the dead letter office," I protested. "And who was there to receive it? Tell me that!"

"I ain't gotta tell you nothin', Stew Meat. Now, if you're all finished with me, I'll get on about my business."

Before I could say another word, he was down the steps and trotting off along the dusty street.

Luther hadn't gone far when he spied our local carpenter, Elias Obern, walking toward him. Elias was toting his tool chest, with a wood saw strapped to its side.

"G'morning, Luther," said Elias. "What brings you out so early this fine day?"

" 'Morning, Mr. Obern. I'm—"

Luther paused. He'd been about to tell Elias how he'd be demonstrating his polish. But why not *show* him instead?

"I'd appreciate a moment of your time, Mr. Obern," he said smoothly. At the same time he poured a dollop of polish on his rag and then set the bottle at the roadside.

"It'll have to be a very brief moment, Luther," Elias replied. "I'm on my way to the Todt place to hang their new front door, and after that—Hey, wait!"

But Luther had already slid the handsaw from its straps. He passed the rag over the blade and handle with swift strokes.

"Luther Gilpin, you put that saw back right now or I'll—" Then Elias was staring at the tool as if seeing it for the first time. "Well if that don't beat all! It looks new as the day I bought it. Seems to be sharper, too. Here. Try that stuff out on my hammer as well."

Luther took the hammer and polished it until it gleamed in the morning sun. "Professor Popkin's Prodigious Polish will shine up anything, Mr. Obern. Just a dollar a bottle, too."

"I've no money just now. But soon as Mrs. Todt pays me for the door, I believe I'd like to buy a bottle of that stuff."

"Yes . . . sir!" replied Luther. He strutted off, whistling a little tune. This was going to be easy!

Working at the forge in his blacksmith shop, Sven Hensen was suddenly greeted by Luther, standing in the doorway. Sven agreed that his largest sledgehammer could use a bit of brightening up.

"Da polish vork like charm," said the blacksmith when Luther had finished. "I think soon maybe I get bottle. Make all dem sledgehammers shine like new ones."

Two bottles practically sold already. Luther was beside himself with happiness.

Prancing out of the shop and looking back over his shoulder at Sven Hensen, he almost bumped into Charlotte Lecky, who was taking a walk with her small daughter, Ruby. Ruby carried a doll crudely fashioned from a pine log, with yarn hair, carpet tacks for eyes, and a great red nose that had once been a wooden bead.

"Land sakes, Luther!" Mrs. Lecky cried out. "Watch where you're going. See, you made Ruby drop her doll."

While the child was still twisting up her face in preparation for a yell of misery, Luther bent down, picked up the grimy doll from the dirt, and passed his rag over its surface.

"Why . . . I never seen the like!" Mrs. Lecky exclaimed. "That thing looks as new as the day my husband made it—better, in fact. Even the chewed places where little Ruby teethed on it are gone. And those little tack eyes seem almost alive. What's on that cloth, Luther?"

He told her. Mrs. Lecky promised to buy a bottle, soon as she collected her egg money.

For a long time, Luther just stood at the edge of the road, considering his good fortune. Three demonstrations, and three promises to buy—he could practically feel the money, rustling and clinking in his pocket already. Professor Popkin sure made a fine product. The polish was practically selling itself.

"I guess I showed ol' Stew Meat a thing or two," muttered Luther to himself. "The way he carried on, you'd think I was doin' the devil's work or something. Ha! What does he know?"

The demonstrating slowed down after that. It was a working day in Coven Tree, and not everybody had either the time or the money to think about buying polish.

Luther, however, did get in a few more licks with that cloth of his.

He heard Shelby Zimmerman taking target practice with his old flintlock rifle out behind the barn. *Flick, flick* went the rag, and the gun gleamed. Shelby swore it seemed to shoot better, too.

Down near Spider Crick, the Widow Vedder was preparing a new vegetable garden. She had her mule hitched to a plow with a badly nicked blade and handles almost black with the grime of years of hard use.

Flick, flick.

The plow might have been delivered just that

day from some farm implement company down in Boston.

On the bench in front of the firehouse, Weldon Davenport was trying his best to whittle a ball-in-a-cage. He'd already ruined three, for his knife was dull. Its blade was caked with rust, the bone handle chipped and loose.

Flick, flick.

Weldon took the knife back from Luther, marveling at its shiny appearance. The glittering blade slid through the wood like a hot wire through a lump of lard.

Naturally Shelby, the Widow Vedder, and Weldon all promised to buy.

WHEEEEEEEEE!

The whistle atop the firehouse announced that it was noon. Luther jammed the cork into the top of the polish bottle and shoved the bottle into a pocket. He'd had enough working for one day.

After all, even the best salesman in the world needed *some* time to relax, didn't he?

While Luther was off doing his demonstrating, back at the farm his ma was getting real worried about Bertram.

All during breakfast the boy sat scratching hard at his right ankle. "It appears to me, young man," said Ma finally, "that you've tromped through some poison ivy. Let me look at that leg."

Before Bertram could protest, Ma drew a chair up beside him, hiked his leg up into her lap, and rolled down his sock.

"Land sakes!" she exclaimed. "What do you make of it, Dorcas?"

Dorcas peered over Ma's shoulder at the fiery welts that dotted Bertram's ankle. They were shaped like little red volcanoes, and in the center of each one was a tiny black dot.

"I never seen the like," Dorcas said. "It's not poison ivy, that's sure. More like he's been pricked by nettles or . . . or . . ."

"What have you gotten into, boy?" Ma asked Bertram. "Did you sneak off to play in Fletcher's bog after I told you a thousand times not to?"

"No, Ma," Bertram mumbled. Then he pressed his lips together tightly. He wasn't about to say one word about how his toy soldiers had been moving around in his room last night. If Ma even suspected him of lying, she was liable to wash out his mouth with her foul-tasting homemade soap.

"D'you want me to get butter and a rag, Miz Gilpin?" Dorcas asked. "So's you can make a poultice? That might prevent an infection."

Hester Gilpin considered this but then shook her head. "This is new to me," she said, "so maybe home remedies aren't the answer. You mind the house, Dorcas, while I take Bertram over to Doc Rush's office."

At that Bertram started whimpering. He didn't want to go to the doctor. Last time he'd been there, Doc Rush had made him swallow a pill that was almost as big as a hen's egg and tasted like an old boot. Even the lollipops Doc always gave him weren't worth going through something like that again.

"Hush up, boy," Ma ordered. "Like it or not, you're seeing the doctor."

At the office, Doc Rush had Bertram sit on a table of polished metal with all kinds of levers and wheels to move the ends up and down. Doc removed Bertram's right shoe and sock to examine the spots. He looked at them from the top and then from the sides. Finally he took a big round magnifying glass from his desk and peered at the boy's leg through it.

"Hmmmm . . . haaa . . . hrumph!"

"What is it, Doc?" asked Ma finally.

"I dunno, Hester. It's new to me. Here, let me try one more thing."

With that, Doc Rush reached into his black bag of shiny instruments. He pulled out a pair of tweezers and a silvery knife that to Bertram's frightened eyes looked as long as a sword.

"He's gonna cut my leg off, Ma!" the boy screamed. "Don't let him do it!"

"You be still," snapped Doc. "I ain't going to cut you. I just want to get a good look at one of those black spots."

While Bertram sobbed and wiped at his nose with the side of one arm, Doc Rush gently scraped the knife across one of the welts until he'd loosened the speck of black at its center. Then he used the tweezers to grasp the thing, which was scarcely as big as the head of a pin. Finally he held up the tweezers and peered through the magnifying glass.

"Hard to believe," he muttered to himself. "It just don't seem possible."

"What, Doc?" Hester asked anxiously. "What don't seem possible?"

Doc Rush didn't seem to hear her. He got up from his stool, still holding the black dot between the jaws of the tweezers, and went to the brass microscope near the window. Placing the dot on a glass slide, he fitted the slide into place and looked through the eyepiece.

"If that don't beat all!" he muttered. "If that don't—"

"Doc Rush, I'm about sick myself, just from worrying!" Hester exclaimed. "If you don't tell me—"

"Here, Hester," said Doc, stepping back to make room for her. "Come see for yourself."

Hester walked across the room and peered into the microscope. "That thing's not like any nettle I ever seen," she said finally. "It's all round, with no pointy end at all."

"What does it look like, Hester?" Doc asked.

Ma closed one eye and squinted again through the brass tube with the other. "This is going to sound real silly, Doc. But that thing resembles nothing so much as one of them round lead balls Shelby Zimmerman fires out of that old-fashioned flintlock rifle of his. Course, I ain't no doctor, and I suppose you've got some other idea."

Doc Rush shook his head. "That's exactly what it looks like to me, too, Hester. I never heard tell of a gun small enough to use a ball the size of the one you're looking at. But if I didn't know better, I'd swear your boy had been shot!"

Luther Gilpin walked briskly through the center of Coven Tree, heading for home. His chest was near busting the buttons loose from his shirt, he was so proud of himself. He'd done exactly what Professor Popkin had ordered. He'd demonstrated the polish to a whole lot of people—all before noon—and every one of 'em had practically promised they'd buy a bottle of it.

Step aside, folks! The best salesman in the world is going home to do a little bragging, and you mustn't get in his way!

He passed the firehouse and the general store and the blacksmith shop, giving each one a grand bow as he passed.

Then, just as he reached the place where the dirt road entered the woods, he heard a man shouting behind him.

"Help, everybody! My ax has gone mad! We've got to do something or it'll chop up every bit of wood in the whole state! Help! Help!"

A woman's shrill scream split the air. "An' my stove, too, an' the broom! The one won't stop heating, and the other won't stop sweeping!"

Luther spun about. There, right in front of the general store, stood Arvid Quist and his wife, Hazel. A crowd of people gathered quickly. In its midst, the Quists waved their hands in the air and yelled loud enough to wake the dead.

"It's like they was alive! We've got to stop 'em before they bring down the shed and the house itself. In all the history of mankind, there never was an ax and a stove and a broom that carried on so, without nobody guiding 'em. Please help us. *Please!*"

An ax? A stove? A broom? Why, thought Luther, those were the three things I polished when I was out there at the Quist house yesterday. But what could be . . . ?

Quickly he yanked the bottle of Professor Popkin's Prodigious Polish from its sack. The picture of Professor Popkin on the label smiled at him. But now the smile was a kind of a leer, as if the professor were mocking him.

Way down at the bottom of the label, some words in tiny print seemed to leap out at Luther. They were the same words he'd seen on the paper that'd blown against his leg two weeks ago.

". . . bring New Life to household objects."

New life! But could that possibly mean . . . ?

Oh, no!

CHAPTER SIX

It Brings New Life

All those people crowding around Arvid and Hazel Quist couldn't make much sense of what the two of 'em were yelling about. That stuff about an ax and a stove and a broom sounded like so much nonsense.

Still, it was clear *something* was going on out at the Quist house. So off everybody went to see what in tarnation it was.

Keeping a little distance from the mob up ahead, Luther followed. His hands were trembling, and though the day was cool, he could feel sweat popping out on his brow. In its cloth bag, the bottle of Professor Popkin's Prodigious Polish suddenly seemed as heavy as a bar of lead.

As they approached the house, everybody heard the sound of chopping, which rang out clear and strong.

Chunk . . . chunk . . . chunk . . .

Rounding the last bend of road, they saw the house itself. There was smoke billowing out of the chimney in great black clouds.

"I ain't put wood in the stove since yesterday suppertime," Hazel Quist bawled.

"And just wait till you see how my ax is carrying on," added her husband.

The sight the crowd beheld as they reached the backyard made all eyes pop near out of their sockets. One or two people screamed loudly, and Mrs. Benthorn fell swooning to the ground.

The ax, all polished and new-looking, was poised in midair over the great mound of firewood Arvid Quist had piled up. Just a few of the logs remained whole. Most of them had been hewed into tiny bits, fit only for matchsticks or perhaps toothpicks.

The ax rose high, as if held by something invisible, and then drove itself deep into yet another log.

Chunk

The log split in two, and with a few quick chops it was reduced to kindling.

"It can't be!" Mayor Eli Phipps cried out. "How can an ax fly about like that, with nobody holding it?"

"How long's it been acting this way, Arvid?" Sheriff Roscoe Houck asked.

"It's hard to say," Arvid told him. "This morning, Hazel and I slept until almost noon. That's strange in itself, for we're accustomed to rising early to get the heavy work done before the heat of the day sets in."

Standing a little off from the rest of the people, Luther remembered Professor Popkin predicting that the Quists would sleep late. But how could he have known . . . ?

"I'd just finished shaving," Arvid went on, "when I heard Hazel in the kitchen, yelling about the stove and the broom. When I came to see what the matter was, there was the broom, sweeping hard enough to wear a hole through the floor. And we couldn't get near the stove because of the heat it was throwing off. Through the window I could see my ax, chopping away as if possessed by the devil himself."

Luther cringed when Arvid mentioned the devil. Meanwhile the ax continued its constant *chunk . . . chunk . . .*

"We came running into town to seek help," Hazel Quist exclaimed. "Now you've got to do something, sheriff, else that stove will burn the house down."

"Hmmm." Sheriff Houck scratched his head. "Seems to me we'd better tend to the ax first, Miz Quist. It's near finished chopping up the woodpile. And the only other wooden things hereabouts are your house and barn. If it goes to work on them, you'll be in real trouble.

"But how are you going to—"

Before she could go on, Sheriff Houck began tiptoeing toward the ax like he was sneaking up on a skittish horse. The ax paid him no mind. It just kept chopping away.

Then, just as the ax started in on yet another chunk of wood, the sheriff lunged. He sprawled across the woodpile with the ax handle gripped tightly in both hands.

The ax lurched and struggled in his grip like some wild animal. All at once the handle slipped out of his sweaty hands. The ax rose into the air, its glittering head poised directly over the sheriff's neck.

With a loud cry, Sheriff Houck rolled to one side, just as the ax came crunching down.

Chunk

The blade bit deep into an oak log. Sheriff Houck sprang to his feet and rushed back to the mass of people in the side yard.

"That thing's stronger'n I am," he told Mayor Phipps. "Somebody's going to get hurt if we aren't careful. Still, we've got to stop it somehow."

Chunk . . . chunk . . . Left to its work, the ax paid the people no mind. It continued chopping at the wood, rising and falling steadily.

"Got any ideas, Roscoe?" the mayor asked.

"Yep. I believe I do. Arvid, have you got any rocks around here?"

"Rocks are one thing my farm raises in abundance," said Arvid. "You'll find 'em aplenty in that field yonder."

"All right, all you folks," the sheriff bawled. "Come with me."

The crowd followed Roscoe, giving the swinging ax a wide berth. Over in the plowed field, the sheriff barked out his orders.

"Each of you get a big rock," he told them. "But not so big that you can't toss it ten or a dozen feet. We'll fix that consarned ax."

When everybody'd located their own special rock, Roscoe led them back and formed them in a big circle around the ax, which kept pumping up and down, up and down, driven by some mysterious energy.

"I guess it can't hear or see us," said Roscoe,

"or it would have attacked long before this. But don't get too close, for that thing's a real danger. Now on the count of three, I want everybody to throw their rocks at it—all at the same time. One . . . two . . . three!"

Several dozen rocks went flying through the air. A lot of 'em dropped short, and many more missed the ax. But one or two struck their target.

Clank

The ax reeled in its downward stroke and tumbled to the ground. "Come on!" the sheriff shouted. "Let's hold it down!"

He leaped onto the fallen ax, and several others did the same. Beneath them the ax trembled and struggled, but the weight of all those people pressing down was just too much for it.

"Take care you don't grasp the cutting edge," Roscoe panted. "It's sharp. The rest of you folks, go get those rocks. Pile 'em on top of this thing. We'll see how lively that ax is when it's buried beneath a few tons of stone."

And so it was done. Within moments, the place where the ax lay was covered with a rock pile taller than a grown man.

"There now," Roscoe puffed when they'd finished. "That ax won't move until Judgment Day unless someone's fool enough to move those rocks. Let's go see about the broom and the stove."

The mass of people gathered about the steps to the kitchen. Roscoe went up to the door and threw it open.

He was met by the old corn broom, sweeping busily at an already spotless floor as if it were held by some dirt-hating housewife. Yet it was moving by itself. Back and forth—back and forth. At the same time a blast of heated air issued from the doorway.

With an impatient shake of his head, Roscoe grasped the broom handle in both hands. Quick as a wink he brought the stick down across his knee.

Snap   The handle broke in two.

Roscoe tucked the two broom pieces under his arm. He could feel them struggle, but they weren't nearly as strong as the ax had been. Over in the corner of the kitchen, the old wood stove glowed a dull red, and the whole room was as hot as a hayloft in mid-August.

Taking the iron lifter from its place on the wall, Roscoe pried up one of the stove lids. Inside, great tongues of flame made a roaring sound. He stuffed the two pieces of broom inside and replaced the lid.

"So much for the ax and the broom," he said. "Now we'll just see about this stove."

He went back to the kitchen door and shouted outside. "Look around and find buckets, cans, dishes—anything that'll hold water," he ordered. "Fill 'em at the well there. Then come inside."

"But sheriff, how could there be a fire in the stove," asked Hazel Quist, "without somebody feeding wood into it?"

"Probably the same way an ax chops wood without anyone holding it," replied Roscoe. "All I know, Miz Quist, is that the stove is doing what stoves do—heating up the place. Here, you folks. Come in here with that water. And Arvid—you fetch a sledgehammer and crowbar and have 'em ready."

Several men and women gathered in the kitchen. Each was holding a container filled with cool water from the well. At Roscoe's direction, they came as near the stove as the withering heat would allow.

"Here's how we'll do it," said the sheriff. "When I tell you, you all pour your water over the stove. Then step away to make room for others to come in and pour more water."

He turned to Arvid Quist. "Arvid, soon as we get the stove cool enough to get close, you start prying it apart with your crowbar. Bust it a few licks with the sledge, if you have to. When something comes loose, take it outside, right away. And keep all the pieces well separated. I don't guess it'll keep burning when it ain't a stove no more."

With that, he signaled to the first group of water carriers. They stepped up and poured the contents of their buckets over the glowing metal.

Hissssssssssssss   Crackkk

Clouds of steam filled the little kitchen. At the same time the stove's top, cooled by the water on top while still red-hot beneath, snapped clean in two. Arvid, his hands thickly wrapped in blankets, grasped one of the pieces, yanked it free with a loud popping of metal fasteners, and threw it out into the yard.

Another bunch of people with pails and cans approached the stove.

Hissssssss

This time Arvid managed to pry one side of the stove loose. "Careful there," snapped Roscoe. "Be ready to wet down any coals that get on the floor. We don't want the house to catch fire."

Strangely enough however, as the stove came apart and the flames inside got lower, there didn't seem to be any coals. The fire had no fuel—it was just . . . *there.*

Finally, with much wetting down of the stove, Arvid Quist managed to break it apart and strew the sections about the side yard. In the kitchen itself, his wife gazed sadly at the soaked floor.

"The place is a mess—just a mess!" she almost sobbed. "It'll take weeks to clean it up, to say nothing of putting in a new stove. I just don't understand. It was like we'd been bewitched or something. What could have caused all this, Sheriff Houck?"

Standing just outside the kitchen window, Luther Gilpin was sure he alone knew the answer to that question. It was all the work of Professor Popkin.

The night brings out a unique feature of my polish.

The professor had said those very words during their buggy ride. But only now did Luther realize their true meaning. Let any object spend one night coated with the magic polish, and the following day, it would take on a life of its own—just as the label on the bottle said.

So *that* was why the professor'd been in such a hurry to have him do his demonstrations. He had to be finished before the polished articles started moving on their own.

Luther looked about. All over the yard stood the people of Coven Tree—his friends and neighbors. Why, the Quists themselves had been ever so nice to him, especially that winter he was sick with the croup. And how had he repaid such kindness?

Through the kitchen window he could see the soggy mass that was the ruin of Hazel Quist's fancy braided rug and the battered stovepipe that hung from its socket in the wall, dribbling bits of soot. He sniffed the foul smells of damp wood and wallpaper. Turning his head, he looked first at the pieces of stove spread about the yard and then at the huge pile of rocks beneath which the ax was imprisoned.

He was the reason for this whole mess—he and Professor Popkin's Prodigious Polish. And soon, all the other things he'd polished would begin to . . .

With a single loud cry of misery, Luther Gilpin ran away from the house and across the fields of the farm. As his astonished neighbors stared after him, he plunged into the thick forest that surrounded the village of Coven Tree.

"Stew Meat? Stew Meat, are you in there?"
It was well after nine o'clock at night, and I

was in the back room of my store working on the day's accounts and shaking my head over the wondrous and terrible events that day at the Quist house when I heard the knocking. Taking up my lantern, I made my way to the front door and opened it.

There stood Dorcas Taney. Her face was pale, and she looked near to busting out crying.

"Oh, Stew Meat," she gasped. "I was hopin' you'd still be about."

"What are you doing out so late?" I asked her.

"It . . . it's Luther," she moaned. "He left the house early this morning, and he hasn't been home since. His folks and me, we're all purely frantic. Mr. Gilpin's walking the main road to see if he can catch sight of Luther, but I know a few special places where he sometimes goes when he's feeling low-down, so I went off on my own."

"Feeling low-down?" I asked.

"I believe he's holding himself responsible for what went on out at the Quist place today. Oh, we heard all about it. Gossip travels right quick in Coven Tree."

"It was eerie, and that's a fact. But why should Luther take the blame on his shoulders?"

With that, Dorcas poured out the whole story about how Luther'd demonstrated Professor

Popkin's Prodigious Polish to the Quists. "I was right there when he did it, Stew Meat," she ended up. "He polished the ax and the stove and the broom. And just a day later, all three was acting like things alive."

It was on the tip of my tongue to tell Dorcas that I'd warned Luther about the polish. But it was plain that was the last thing she wanted to hear. She had a special feeling for the lad and wanted only to help him if she could.

"Why come to me?" I asked.

"I believe I can find Luther. Talking him into coming home is something else. But you're the best talker in this town, Stew Meat. You could sell ice to an Eskimo. You have to convince him that running off isn't an answer to his problems."

With that, she began to sob as if her heart was breaking.

I'm like most men, and a woman's tears can make me do about anything. Besides, here in Coven Tree, we have a habit of helping one another. I slipped on a sweater against the cool night air and took up my lantern, and we were off.

Luther wasn't in the big hollow tree at the base of Old Baldy mountain, nor did we find him in the cave near old Magda the witch's shanty. For two hours we looked high and low, with nary a sign of the boy.

"Just one place left," said Dorcas. She led me along the bank of Spider Crick until we came to a spot where the tree branches bent out over the bank like the roof of a thatched cottage.

Sure enough, we heard a rustling from beneath the branches. "Luther?" called Dorcas, while I hoped we hadn't disturbed a skunk or even a bear. "Luther, is that you?"

"Dorcas?" came the reply in a wretchedly sad voice. "What are you doin' out here this time of night?"

"I . . . we . . . we came to take you home, Luther," she said. "Where you belong."

There was some more rustling, and then Luther came out from under the branches and into the light of the lantern. His hair was all mussed, and his best clothes were grimy with dirt, and from the look of his eyes he'd been crying more than somewhat.

"I ain't going back home," he said. "Never."

"But you got to, Luther. Your parents are all upset, and they need you to help work the farm, and I thought you might be hurt or even . . . even . . ."

"How can I go back and face folks in town after what I done?" Luther replied miserably. "Maybe I'll run off to some other place where nobody ever heard of me. Or maybe I'll just stay here and starve to death. Now leave me be!"

Dorcas was about to speak up again when I gripped her arm in a signal to be silent. "Let's do as he wants, Dorcas," I said. "If he's got his mind made up, who are we to change it? I surely am disappointed though."

A strange look came across Luther's face. "Disappointed? What do you mean by that, Stew Meat?"

"Not long ago, Luther Gilpin, you was telling me how you'd one day be the greatest salesman who ever was. But it appears to me that when the goin' gets rough, you ain't got the nerve to do what's right."

"I *am* doing what's right," Luther insisted. "I'm running off, so people don't have to put up with me no more."

"Running off is easy," I told him. "It's the coward's way."

"I may be a lot of awful things, but I ain't no coward."

"No? Luther, down in my store, I've sold lots of things that didn't turn out the way people expected. Why, once Elmer Baggot ordered a fine, go-to-meeting buggy that I sent all the way to Boston for. But first time he tried it out, the single-tree split and one wheel fell off. An' just the other day, Ellen Huckabee bought what she thought was a box of raisins, to decorate a cake for her quilting party. Only somebody'd sneaked back when I wasn't looking and opened the box real careful and ate all the raisins and filled it with cornmeal. What do you think I do when things like that happen, Luther?"

"I . . . I suppose you have to make it good with your customers," he mumbled.

"That's right. I lost a pile of money on Elmer's wagon, for he canceled his order, and the factory wouldn't bear the cost of returning it. And it was weeks before Ellen Huckabee forgave me for making her look like a fool at her quilting bee. But did I sneak off into the woods and go to feeling sorry for myself?"

"I . . . I expect not," Luther mumbled.

"Selling's not all sunshine and roses," I said. "And when things go wrong, the seller's got to do the right thing. D'you think you're really doing the right thing by crouching here in the dark, Luther?"

"N . . . no."

"And there's something else, too. I suspect the ax and stove and broom out at the Quist place weren't the only things you demonstrated your polish on. Think about that, boy."

"I know," replied Luther with a groan. "It'll start tomorrow morning."

Then, suddenly, a frightened look came across his face. "Pa's awl and Bertram's soldiers!" he cried out. "I polished them two days ago. They must be acting up already."

"Well, that explains a good deal," said Dorcas with a nod of satisfaction. "Like how your brother got them tiny bullets in his ankle. But you don't need to worry about the soldiers, Luther. Bert told us how he'd burned 'em in the stove."

"And the awl?"

"I was in the toolroom this morning, looking for a tack hammer," Dorcas replied. "I saw that awl driven into a hardwood log about as far as it would go, and I wondered why your pa would do such a thing. Now I know. But that awl won't move again until doomsday unless someone splits it out of the wood."

"But I demonstrated the polish in town, too. Oh, how am I going to face people when their possessions start moving like living things?"

"If you've got any courage at all, Luther," I told

him, "you've got to go back and make good on what you did, like any real salesman would. Sure, folks'll be angry at first. But we're mighty forgiving here in Coven Tree. And this isn't the first time Old Nick has tried to have his way with us."

Dorcas stared at me wide-eyed and put her hand to her lips. "Stew Meat!" she gasped. "D'you think the Devil himself is—"

"What other creature could concoct a polish that brings things to life?" I asked. "We'll beat him, though, just as we've done before, if Luther's got the sand in him to go back and—"

"I'll come with you," Luther said. "I expect it'll be hard, with everybody scorning and hating me for what I done."

"I'll not scorn nor hate you," I told him. "For there's no meanness in you. You're just a lad who got tempted by the greatest tempter of all. And now that you know the way of things, you'll mend what you've broken."

"I'm your friend too, Luther," said Dorcas. She grasped his hand and held it tightly. "No matter what comes of this, I'll always be your friend."

With that, the three of us began making our way back to town, each with the same question in mind . . .

What would the morning bring?

CHAPTER SEVEN

Courage and Mischief

It was in the wee hours of the morning that Luther and Dorcas and I arrived back at the Gilpin house. There were lights in all the windows, and we could see Simon and Hester, sitting and waiting for word about their son.

First thing Hester did when Luther entered was give him a big hug and kiss. Right after that, she boxed his ears for running off and scaring 'em half to death. Finally she brewed coffee and made us tell all about what had been going on.

"Strange doings," she said when she'd heard our tale of how the polish had been the cause of all the trouble over at the Quist place.

"The Devil's work, to be sure," added Luther's pa. "I hope you've learned your lesson, Luther, and you'll have no more to do with that Professor Popkin or his magic polish."

"I won't be selling it no more, and that's a fact," Luther replied. "Only . . ."

"Only what, Luther?" asked Simon and Hester together.

The lad hung his head in shame and mumbled something none of us could understand. "Speak up boy," Hester commanded.

At that, Luther poured out the whole story about how he'd spent the morning demonstrating his polish throughout Coven Tree.

"Now Luther'll be going back to town to put things right again," I said when he'd finished.

"D'you think Luther'll be in any danger?" Hester gasped.

"Safe or not, Hester, it's up to Luther to do what's right," said Simon. "That's the way we taught him. But if my son needs any help when he confronts those . . ."

Luther shook his head firmly. "I'm the one that brought on all this trouble. And I'm the one who's got to mend it."

"I could use a bit of rest and another cup of your coffee, Hester," I said. "There's been no sleep at all for me this night, and I'm a bit weary."

"But Stew Meat," Luther protested, "shouldn't

we be off to town before the polish gets to working its magic?"

"No," I said with a little shake of my head. "Seems to me that if we show up in the dark hours with a wild story about Professor Popkin's Polish, folks'll just think our wits are addled. We'd best wait until morning, when the enchantment will begin, but before there's time for any real damage. Then, Luther, you and I can—"

"You two?" Dorcas exploded. "What about me?"

"You'd be better off here," Luther told her. "No telling what those tools and things will do when they get to prancing around. I'd be afraid that you—"

"Mebbe you'd be afraid," snapped Dorcas, "but I'm not! I'm going with you, Luther Gilpin!"

Luther looked about helplessly. "Ma? Pa? Can you talk some sense into this girl?"

Hester glanced at Simon, and a little grin curled the corners of her mouth. "There's no reasoning with Dorcas when she's got her mind set on something," Hester said. "You'd best let her come, Luther."

The rising sun was perched on the horizon like an orange on a plate when the three of us set off for Coven Tree. As we reached the village, a loud clanging started in the blacksmith's shop.

"That'll be Sven Hensen," I said. "Let's go see what's happening to that polished hammer of his."

At his anvil, Sven was working on a plow point with a dirty, smudged hammer. The one Luther had polished was resting on a bench in the corner.

We greeted Sven, but we couldn't take our eyes off the gleaming tool. "When was it you shined that thing up?" I asked Luther.

"Yesterday," he replied. "I was up real early to do my demonstrating."

"Vhat are you folks vhispering about?" Sven asked. "Iss sometin' going on I should know?"

"Mebbe you'd better stop work for a bit," I told him. "Just keep your eye on the hammer there."

"Vhy? You afraid dat hammer gonna sit up and—"

Then—while Sven was still talking—the hammer *did* sit up!

"Hey!" shouted the blacksmith. "Vhat's goin' on here? Hammer shouldn't move unless I move it!"

Without warning, the hammer flew through the air and poised itself over the anvil. It pounded down on the heavy plow point, which rang like a bell.

Before Luther or Dorcas or I could act, Sven snatched up a long length of chain that was hanging from a nail. Holding it by one end, he snapped it at the hammer as if it were a whip. The flying end of the chain wrapped itself around the hammer, which began struggling like a thing alive. Using all his great strength, Sven dragged the hammer to the floor. Then he put both his feet solidly on top of it.

"Now, one of you tell me vhat's happening here," he commanded.

Luther told Sven about Professor Popkin's Prodigious Polish and the trouble it was causing. At the same time, Dorcas found a clean rag in a drawer of the workbench.

"I'll just wash away all the polish," she said, dipping the rag into the barrel of water near the forge. "Then the hammer should be back to normal again."

Kneeling down at Sven's feet, she scrubbed away at the handle and head, and even used dirt from the floor to scrape away the polish. Sven shifted his feet so she could get to all parts of the hammer. "There now," she said at length. "That should do it."

Sven removed his feet. The hammer wriggled out of the chain wrapped about it, leaped back into the air over the anvil, and began pounding away.

"It didn't work!" Dorcas exclaimed. "I scoured that thing, hard as I could. But the polish won't come off. What are we going to do now?"

"I show you vhat I do," said Sven. From his bench he plucked up the long-handled pincers he used to hold metal in the forge for heating. Then he extended the pincers toward the hammer and squeezed mightily.

Like capturing a flying insect, Sven grabbed the hammer even as it was rising for another blow. The jaws of the pincers clamped together just where the hammer's handle and head were connected. The hammer struggled in the grip, and Sven's great arm was jerked to and fro. But the blacksmith managed to haul the hammer over to his forge, where a mound of charcoal glowed red in the brick furnace box.

Sven jammed the hammer in among the hot coals and held it firmly with the pincers. In the intense heat, the handle first charred and then burst into flame. For a few moments we could see the hammer head struggling to escape as its metal changed color from silver to a red glow.

Finally, however, it was still. "Ain't no hammer gonna get de best of me!" the blacksmith announced.

Before Sven could say another word, we dashed outside. Luther headed for the shed where Elias Obern did much of his carpentry work, with Dorcas and me following after. As we approached, we could hear the sounds of sawing and pounding, along with Elias's yells.

"Hey, there! You stop that now! You're cutting up all my best wood and pounding nails into everything. Stop it, I say!"

Sure enough, the saw was working its way through long boards of pine, making helter-skelter cuts, while the hammer rooted around in the nail box for yet another spike to hammer into the surface of the workbench. Elias was prancing around the shed like his pants were afire, screaming at the tools.

Luther threw himself at the saw, grasping its handle while the blade was deep in the pile of boards. He yanked the handle sideways, hard as he could, and the blade buckled and twisted. The saw began struggling like a thing alive. But it was trapped in the kerf it had cut into the wood.

At the same time, Dorcas grabbed the shingle hatchet and a long rafter nail. She pushed the struggling hammer down upon the bench and pressed the point of the nail against the tool's wooden handle.

Pow Pow Pow

With the back of the hatchet, she drove the nail clear through the hammer handle and deep into the bench top. After wiping the sweat from her brow, she pounded home two more nails. That hammer wouldn't be moving again until Judgment Day.

"And you thought I couldn't help, Luther Gilpin," she panted. "How about that?"

No time for making any explanations to Elias Obern. We were off to the Lecky house, where a little girl named Ruby had a very special doll.

"Oh, I'm so glad you three came," Ruby's ma, Charlotte, cried when we got there. "Ruby's wooden doll climbed that old crabapple tree out back, and it won't come down for anything. I know I'm talking silly, but it happened. It really did!"

"We know, Miz Lecky," I said. "An' we're here to put things right."

In the backyard, Ruby was beneath the crabapple tree, crying her eyes out. Up in the branches we could see her little doll, peering out from among the leaves and blinking its tiny carpet-tack eyes.

Luther began climbing the tree. At the same time, Dorcas found an old burlap sack in the woodshed and stood below, holding the sack's neck wide.

As Luther climbed, the doll climbed higher. Finally, however, it reached a branch that was too supple to hold it. Down it tumbled—straight into Dorcas's sack.

Dorcas clasped her hands about the neck of the sack. "Get me a piece of twine, Ruby," she ordered. When Ruby fetched the twine, Dorcas tied it about the sack's neck. Inside, the doll struggled and flailed about like a trapped animal.

"Hang this in the barn somewhere," Dorcas told Mrs. Lecky, handing her the sack. "Above all, don't untie it, whatever happens."

"But I want my dolly!" wailed Ruby.

"Not that one, you don't," I said, trying to comfort the girl. "But tell you what. Next time you're down to my store, I'll give you a dolly that'll make that ol' wooden one look like nothing at all. It won't cost you a cent. The doll in my store is near as big as you are, and it's all stuffed cloth, with a red-checked dress and—"

"Ohhh, Stew Meat!" Ruby cried with a wide smile.

We headed toward the Zimmerman place. "It's real nice of you to give Ruby that new doll for free, Stew Meat," said Luther.

"To Ruby, it's free," I told him. "You'll be paying for it, Luther, soon as you earn the money. I'm glad to help you out in your time of need, but business is business."

Bang While we were still a ways off, we could hear the sound of Shelby Zimmerman's flintlock gun firing.

Bang Bang

"The gun's firing faster'n any flintlock should," said Luther. "A muzzle loader takes a heap of preparation before each shot."

Out behind the barn, Shelby stood staring down at his rifle, which was lying with its barrel across a mound of dirt. *Bang* Even as we watched, it fired again.

"Target practice," said Shelby. "All by it-self, without me loading or priming or any-thing. A bull's-eye every time. I never seen the like."

"It'll go on forever if we don't stop it," I told him. "And somebody taking a walk out there by your target could be hurt."

"It is kind of interesting, though, how it keeps

shooting that way," said Shelby. "Been going on for the better part of an hour. But stopping it's no problem."

With that he took a dirty handkerchief from his pocket, stepped up behind the rifle, and wadded the cloth about the hammer, where a bit of flint was clutched between viselike jaws. "It won't fire so long as the flint can't strike the metal plate. But what do you make of all this, Stew Meat? How's it happening?"

"No time for explanations now, Shelby. Just keep that handkerchief tied tight and the gun locked away. We've got to be off to see the Widow Vedder."

By this time, things that moved by themselves were getting to be an old story. At the Vedder place the widow was standing in her side yard, yelling and screaming fit to bust. Her plow was cutting through the ground smoothly and steadily, with no horse or mule to pull it. It had already turned over the earth in the whole vegetable garden and much of the backyard. When we arrived, it was just starting in on her patch of prize marigolds.

Luther ran past the Widow Vedder, grabbed the handles of the plow, and wrestled it to the ground.

Then Dorcas picked up a heavy stone, while I got another. We pounded at that plow until it was nothing more than a pile of wood and metal bits, lying on the earth.

"I expect you've got enough land turned over for this year," Luther told the astounded Widow Vedder. "An' I'm sure Stew Meat'll be glad to replace your plow with a new one."

I gave Luther a questioning look over the tops of my glasses. "I . . . I'd be glad to buy it for you, ma'am," he finished lamely.

Five down, and one to go. In front of the firehouse we found Weldon Davenport on his feet and staring at the bench on which he usually sat. The bench was now whittled out in a manner that might bring envy to the heart of a Swiss wood-carving master. The arms, once nothing but pine planks, had been worked into a lacy filigree, and on the back was a picture of Washington crossing the Delaware, with the figures looking so real you expected them to start talking. Weldon's knife, working its way through the wood all by itself, was making a copy of a Rembrandt painting on the seat and doing a fine job of it.

"Weldon," I said, "we got to do something about that knife."

"Aww, Stew Meat," he protested. "Can't you wait until it's finished here? Those pictures are pretty as anything."

"Nope. As far as I know, that knife'll whittle from now to doomsday unless it's stopped. It'd turn the whole firehouse into latticework if we'd let it."

While I was talking to Weldon, Luther took a handkerchief from his pocket and wrapped it about the palm of his hand. Then he grasped the knife and threw it to the ground. Finally he placed his foot on the blade and yanked upward on the handle. The blade snapped clean off.

Gingerly the boy picked up the blade. "I'll just take this back over to Sven Hensen's forge," he said. "I reckon an hour or two among the coals there will calm it down some."

And so the ruination that Luther Gilpin—and Professor Popkin's Prodigious Polish—had almost brought to Coven Tree was overcome. Luther, Dorcas, and I returned to my store, where I told the waiting customers to come back some other time. Once inside, I opened three bottles of homemade root beer so we could celebrate our victory.

Victory? Not hardly.

Y'see, while we were rescuing the folks of the

village from Luther's folly, we had no idea what his young brother Bertram was getting into back at the Gilpin place.

Bertram sat on a stump in his backyard, rubbing at the bandage Ma had wrapped on his ankle after she'd picked the tiny bullets from beneath his skin with a needle and washed the area with her lye soap. He was bored—especially now, with Luther away, Ma and Pa on the front porch awaiting his return, and no soldiers to play with.

What was there to do? Luther was lucky, Bertram thought to himself. He could go off day or night, showing folks how to use that stuff in the bottle.

Then he had an idea. If Luther could go gallivanting around with that polish, why couldn't he? Maybe he'd even sell a bottle or two. Then Luther'd be proud of him, all right.

He walked over to the barn and into the toolroom. Sure enough, there was the crate. He peered inside. The bottles stood there in their rows, with just the one missing. They seemed to be almost inviting him to pick one up.

He did. The cork was stuck tight, and for a minute he thought about cracking the neck off the bottle by busting it on a rock. No, that wouldn't do. He needed something with a sharp point to pry out the cork.

He saw the awl, jammed tight in the log, and tried to pull it free. It was stuck. Well, a nail would be almost as good.

Half an hour later, he finally had a hole bored down to the polish. Bits of cork floated on the liquid's surface, but that didn't make any difference. Bertram found a piece of rag and went out of the barn and across the fields, whistling happily to himself.

It wasn't long before he saw the bell tower of the Coven Tree School, looming over the tops of the trees. He'd been inside the school just once. That was last spring, when Ma had registered him. A few more weeks, though, and he'd be going there as a brand-new first grader. But now the place was deserted for the summer.

As Bertram stared at the tower, an idea suddenly popped into his head. The old bell hanging up there was all dingy and green from being out in the weather. It could use a good shining up. And he had the stuff to do it, too.

He approached the building, more than a little scared. If somebody caught him sneaking about and told his parents, Ma'd give him a paddling he'd never forget.

He went to the front door and tried it. It was locked. He was just about to give up and go home when he spotted the busted window, just above the big heap of stovewood piled up for the coming winter. It was almost as if somebody'd been expecting him to try and get inside.

He climbed the pile of wood, stuck his hand through the broken pane, and turned the latch. Then, with yet another look around, he raised the window and climbed inside.

It was the fifth- and sixth-grade classroom. Bertram had never been in here before. He sat at one of the desks, wondering if he'd ever grow big enough to fit something that large.

But say—he hadn't come in just to sit where the bigger boys and girls did!

He found the door to the bell tower and tried it, half hoping it'd be locked so he could forget about his plan and go home without the chance of getting into trouble. But the door swung open at his first touch.

He climbed the narrow stairs to the trapdoor at the top. Pushing the trapdoor open, he hauled himself up into the tower itself.

Why, from here he could see just about all of Coven Tree. There was the church and the firehouse and Stew Meat's store. And over yonder he spotted the lumber mill and Doc Rush's office and the abandoned Fiske farm.

Next to him hung the bell. It was almost as tall as Bertram himself, and a lot bigger around. He rubbed his hand against the metal surface and wrinkled his nose at the dust and grime that came off on his palm. He'd fix that soon enough.

Taking the bottle of Professor Popkin's Prodigious Polish from his pants pocket, he gave the rag a good soaking. Then he started rubbing on the bell.

In just a few minutes the great bell glittered in coppery splendor, both inside and out. "Just wait till folks see that," Bertram murmured to himself. After a last look around, he went back downstairs, out through the window, and back into the woods.

Bertram walked on among the trees until he came to a large structure that seemed to be all roof and no walls. The roof was held in place simply by wooden poles spaced along its edge every six feet or so.

It was the sawmill. But there were no workmen around. They were off in the woods somewhere with their teams of strong-backed horses, gathering up the logs to be sawed into planks.

Bertram crept in under the roof. At one end of the building sat the great steam engine that powered the saw. The firebox was freshly cleaned, and the boiler shone like a brand-new dime. No need for polishing here.

Then the enormous saw caught the boy's eye. The legs of the table on which it sat were as big around as pickle barrels, and the surface was of planks a full four inches thick. It stood higher than Bertram himself.

In the center of the table, mounted on massive fittings, the blade of the great saw sat like an enormous round idol. Underneath, the huge steel circle almost touched the floor. Above, it missed the ceiling rafters by mere inches. All around the circle, great notches, like the teeth of dragons, stood ready to screech and whine their way through the biggest and hardest of logs.

Now, however, the blade was still. And it was dirty, covered with pine pitch.

Bertram climbed up one leg of the immense table and hauled himself onto its surface. With a last look about, he dampened his rag again from the bottle and set to work.

When he'd finished both sides of the saw's top, he tried moving the blade to get at the bottom. Pressing his hands flat against both sides, and being careful not to cut himself on the razor-sharp teeth, he pressed downward.

As massive as the blade was, it turned easily. The saw's clean hemisphere moved down, and the dirty one came up to take its place. Again Bertram set to work with his rag.

With the blade all covered with polish, Bertram turned his attention to the table itself. After shining the upper surface, he climbed back down to the floor and worked on the bottom, the legs, the supports, and—

"What are you doin' in here, boy?"

The loud voice startled Bertram, and he almost dropped his rag and bottle as he looked about to see where it was coming from.

Over in one corner of the structure stood a bearded, grizzled man in a red-checked shirt. "I said what are you doing hereabouts? Don't you know it's dangerous to . . ."

Then the man looked at the saw. "Did you do that, boy?" he rumbled. "By yourself?"

"Yes . . . yes, sir," said Bertram. "But don't get mad at—"

"I ain't mad, boy. I just marvel that one young'un could shine that thing up better'n my men could do if they went at it all day. What's your name?"

"Bertram. Bertram Gilpin."

"Oh, yes. You'd be Simon and Hester's lad. I'll bet they'd hang your hide out for the crows if they knew you'd been playing about here. It's a risky place, even for grown men. Well I'm going to make you a little deal, Bertram Gilpin."

"What . . . what kind of a deal?"

"You go along home and promise me you'll never play here again. In return—since you shined up the saw so grand—I won't tell your folks what you've been up to."

Bertram breathed a long sigh of relief. He crammed the bottle into his pocket, darted out from beneath the roof, and ran off through the woods toward home.

Behind him, the great saw sat solidly on its table. Both saw and table were covered from top to bottom with Professor Popkin's Prodigious Polish.

CHAPTER EIGHT

The Great
Buzz Saw Battle

During the time Luther'd been having his problems with Professor Popkin's Prodigious Polish, he'd gotten way behind in his farm work. So the next morning found him out in the bean field, plucking weeds. He still held to his dream of getting rich as a salesman, however. It was the first thing he spoke of when Dorcas came out to call him for lunch.

"Of course the polish didn't work out the way I expected," he told her. "But I guess a beginning salesman's got to figure on some setbacks. Someday I'll find me the right product. Then I'll give up the farm for good and make my fortune with my sharp wits and ready tongue."

"Luther Gilpin," she said with a shake of her head, "when are you going to realize how well off you are on this farm? Didn't these last days teach you anything? Look at the mess you caused with your selling."

"I put everything right, didn't I? Everything's back the way it was."

"Hmmph! You owe Stew Meat for the doll and the plow he's replacing, don't you? I'm not sure we're done with things moving by themselves, either. I'm more than a little worried, Luther."

"But why?"

"Think on it. Remember how hard I scrubbed at Sven Hensen's hammer? But that polish just won't wash off. So those tools and the gun and the doll have still got a hex on 'em. To be sure, they're all held down or locked up or whatever. But what happens if they get loose?"

"Then we'll bust 'em up just like the Quists' stove and Widow Vedder's plow. Neither of those things moved, once they were in pieces."

"Perhaps," said Dorcas doubtfully. "I just don't like the idea of hammers and the ax and . . . and especially a *gun*, just waiting their chance to get free and maybe harm folks. There's something else on my mind, too."

"My, ain't you the little bundle of cheer today. What more is troubling you?"

"It's Bertram. He's acting mighty strange, like

he's been up to something and doesn't want any-one to find out."

"He's just moody about the way his soldiers came to life," said Luther. "He'll be fine, soon as I make him another toy to play with. Come on, Dorcas. Take that rain cloud out of your pocket and cheer up."

"I'm sorry. I've just got this uneasy feeling down inside that things ain't right somehow."

As they walked across the fields toward the house, the bonging of the school bell came floating through the air. "That's odd," said Dorcas. "School's out for the summer. Why would any-body—"

"Maybe they're testing it," said Luther. "Or some scamp, up to a little mischief. It's none of our affair."

When they reached the kitchen door, Luther's ma was waiting. She held out a half-used bottle of polish.

"I found this in a sack in the pocket of your best pants when I was readying the wash this morning," she told Luther. "If there's any truth to what you said about your doings in town, you'd best put it away somewhere safe."

Luther took the bottle and headed for the toolroom in the barn to place it in its crate. Moments later he was running back toward the house, and his yells drowned out the pealing of the school bell.

"Ma! Pa! Oh, this is terrible!"

"What's terrible?" Pa asked.

"That . . . that crate in the tool room. There's a bottle in it with a hole picked through the cork."

"D'you mean *another* one? Besides the one you just . . ."

Luther nodded vigorously. "An' it ain't as full as the rest of 'em. Somebody besides me has gotten into that polish."

Ma looked about, just in time to see Bertram sneaking through the door to the front of the house.

"Bertram Gilpin, you come back here this instant!" she commanded sternly.

Bertram slunk back and stood with head bowed before his ma.

"Did you take out a bottle of that polish, boy?" Ma asked. "And then put it back, hopin' we wouldn't notice? The truth now. This is important."

Bertram nodded, looking like he was about to cry.

"Did . . . did you use any of the polish?" demanded Luther.

Again the boy nodded. Luther, his parents, and Dorcas all looked at one another in frightened astonishment. In the silent kitchen, the only sound was the bonging of the school bell.

"The bell!" Dorcas cried out suddenly. "I'll bet that's what Bertram was—"

With that, they all dashed outside and began running across the fields toward the school.

When they got there, quite a crowd had already gathered. They were all looking up at the tower, where the gleaming bell swung back . . . *bong* . . . and forth . . . *bong* . . .

Mayor Eli Phipps caught sight of Luther and came scuttling over importantly. "Luther," said the mayor, "we've all heard of your polish and its disastrous consequences. Now the bell is working by itself, with nobody pulling on the rope. Is this more of the same mischief?"

"Yes, sir," replied Luther miserably. "I suspect it is."

"Then it's up to you to make amends," said the mayor. "How do you intend to do it?"

Luther mulled this over in his mind. Finally he pointed to four of the largest men in Coven Tree, including Packer Vickery, who weighed close to three hundred pounds. "Can they help me?" Luther asked the mayor.

The mayor puffed out his chest, full of self-importance. "You four go with Luther," he ordered, like the idea was his own.

Someone unlocked the door of the school. Luther, followed by his four huge helpers, entered the building. The pealing of the bell crashed into their ears.

"So much sound!" Packer Vickery cried out. "It sets the very walls to shaking. This school will fall down about our ears if we don't do something quick."

Luther yanked open a door. Beside the stairs leading to the bell tower, the heavy bell rope hung down. The loop at its end was rising and falling, yanked by the bell above.

"When I count to three," said Luther, "I want all you men to grab hold of that rope. Put your whole weight on it. D'you understand?"

The men nodded.

"One . . . two . . . *three!*"

The three men grabbed on tight. In their hands the rope jerked like something alive as the bell above them tolled one last time.

BONG

Then . . .

clink

Then silence.

A great cheer arose from outside.

"Tie the rope off, and tie it tight," Luther commanded. "We don't want the bell getting loose again." Even as he spoke, the men could feel the rope quiver as the bell above tried to break free.

They wrapped the rope about a great wooden post next to the stairs and knotted it fast. At the same time there was a sound of footsteps across the wooden floor, and Mayor Phipps appeared in the doorway.

"You've stilled the bell, Luther," said the mayor. "But what's to be done now?"

"What do you mean?" Luther asked.

"We can't have a school bell that rings whenever it feels like it. I suppose it'll have to be taken down and buried. Then a new one must be purchased. The total cost, I expect, will be somewhere around two hundred dollars. And it's your responsibility, Luther Gilpin."

Two hundred dollars! Luther'd never seen anything close to that much money in his life. Why, he'd . . . he'd never get out of debt! Even the best of salesmen couldn't afford that kind of money.

Before he could say a word, there was a cry

from the school yard. "Mayor Phipps—Luther Gilpin! You two had best come out here, right now!"

They went to the schoolhouse door. Outside, the people were gathered about a bearded man wearing boots and heavy work clothes. Sawdust was sprinkled on the man's clothes and in his hair.

"That's Homer Bedlow," said Mayor Phipps. "He's the foreman over at the sawmill. But what's he doing here?"

"I was headed for town when I seen all you people gathered here," gasped Homer. "You got to come and help. We'll need everybody we can get. Oh, it's awful!"

"What's awful, Homer?" bawled someone in the crowd.

"The buzz saw—the great big one. It's running wild!"

"Now take it easy, Homer," said the mayor. "If something's wrong with the saw, just pry the drive belt loose. Or shut down the steam engine. That'll—"

"You don't understand. The belt's still hanging on its peg, and the engine ain't even fired up. The saw's running by itself!"

"What?"

"That's not all. The saw table busted loose from its mountings, and it's hobbling around the woods on those four wooden legs like a horse with spavins. The blade's whirring and slicing at standing trees. We've got to stop it somehow. But none of my men dare get near it!"

With that, the whole mass of people turned and began moving off in the direction of the sawmill like a herd of sheep. Luther, his parents, and Dorcas followed along.

They were still some distance away from the mill when they heard a great whirring whine that reminded Luther of the sound of fingernails scratching on a blackboard. This was followed by the crash of a falling tree. Next, a man's shout:

"Careful, Festus! Don't get in its way. It'll cut you in two!"

The crowd arrived at the sawmill, and all eyes near popped clear out of their heads as they stared at the . . . the *thing* . . . on the far side of the clearing.

The gigantic buzz saw, still mounted on its table, seemed to be looking back at them defiantly. Then, incredibly, the great blade began to move. It began slowly, then gathered speed with a shriek like a dragon in pain.

WHEEEEEEEE

The legs of the table scrabbled in the earth, and the saw made its way to a nearby maple tree a full two feet thick.

WHEEEEEEEE

The front legs kind of splayed out like those of a dog examining a rabbit hole, while the rear ones tipped the table forward. The saw bit into the tree trunk.

WAAAAAAAW WAAAAAAAAW WAAAAAAAW

The saw made several up-and-down cuts in the tree trunk. Finally there was a crackling sound, and the tree, weakened by the cuts, crashed down with a loud thump.

The huge blade came to a halt.

"The blade can't turn itself sideways," Homer Bedlow told the mayor. "Even so, at the rate it's going, it'll have half the trees in the county cut down by nightfall."

Mayor Phipps looked about. "Where's Luther Gilpin?" he shouted.

Luther stepped forward. "And just what are you going to do about that . . . that saw?" the mayor demanded.

It wasn't fair, Luther thought. After all, Bertram had polished the saw. It was all Bert's fault.

But Luther knew that wasn't really true. He, not Bert, was the one who'd ordered the polish from Professor Popkin in the first place. It was up to him to fix things—if he could.

He moved out of the crowd and began walking across the clearing toward the saw. The saw seemed to be sneering at this mere mortal who came to do combat. The great blade began spinning slowly. As Luther got closer, the speed increased.

WHEEEEEEEEE

The saw inched forward. Luther backed away. The saw followed him. Suddenly the wooden legs slammed against the ground like those of a mad-dened bull.

The buzz saw charged at Luther.

Caught by surprise, he sprang to one side, and the saw went screaming by. Luther fumbled among the leaves and twigs on the ground until he found a rock. He hurled it at the spinning blade.

CLANG

The rock bounced off without doing any harm. The saw turned toward Luther again. Luther backed away, and the blade spun to a halt.

"Mayor Phipps!" Luther called across the clearing.

"What is it?" came the answer.

"So long as I keep the saw's attention, it won't be cutting down any trees."

"That's a fine start, lad," said the mayor. "But it still doesn't solve our problem. How are we going to capture that thing?"

"I dunno, sir. Maybe somebody else has an idea."

"I got one," Homer Bedlow offered. "If that thing wants wood, let's give it wood. Maybe we can jam the blade somehow."

With that, Homer began snapping orders at his men. They began gathering logs—the biggest and hardest they could find, full of knots and twists.

Two men at the ends of an oak log almost two feet around approached the saw. The blade began to spin.

"Jam it in there as hard as you can!" said Homer Bedlow.

WHEEEE

Standing on either side of the saw, the men forced the log into its teeth.

WHEEEEE . . . AAAAAWWW . . . WHEEEEE

The saw blade sliced through the hard wood as if it were soft cheese.

"It ain't gonna work, Mayor," said Homer. "If the saw will handle that log, it'll take on anything in the forest."

"But couldn't you try a rock? Or an axhead?"

Homer shook his head. "The teeth won't bite on anything as hard as rock or iron," he told Mayor Phipps. "Even if they did, the blade would likely shatter and explode like a bomb. That'd put everyone in more danger than they are now, to say nothing of having live bits of saw blade lying about the woods."

By this time the saw had turned to face Luther again.

"I can keep you hopping about for some time yet," Luther said. "Only problem is, sooner or later I'll get tired. But you? You don't get tired, do you?"

WHEEEEEEE

All at once the saw lurched about. It seemed to be noticing the crowd at the edge of the clearing for the first time. It shuffled its wooden feet among the leaves.

Then it charged straight at the mass of people.

With screams and shouts of fright and astonishment, everyone went dashing off into the woods where the saw couldn't follow.

All except Dorcas Taney.

She'd been standing with her back against a tree, murmuring something to Hester Gilpin. The saw's charge surprised her. As she turned to flee, a sleeve of her dress caught on a broken limb.

She struggled to free herself. The saw's legs made rustling sounds as it came closer . . . and closer.

"Dorcas! No!"

Without any thought for his own safety, Luther took up a long fallen branch as thick as his wrist and dashed up behind the saw. "Take that, you overgrown eggbeater!" he cried, striking again and again at the spinning blade with his wooden club.

WHEEEEEEEE

With each blow, his branch got shorter and shorter as the teeth sheared off the wood. Dorcas was spattered by thrown sawdust. Then, just as she felt the breeze of the whirring teeth on her cheek, the saw decided it'd taken enough punishment from Luther and turned about.

Seeing Dorcas scuttle safely into the woods, Luther ran to the far side of the clearing, breathing heavily.

"If you're trying to tire me out, you're sure doing a fine job of it," he panted.

Off among the trees, Hester Gilpin moved beside Dorcas. "Luther can't take much more," Dorcas told her.

"I know, lass." Hester's whole body was trem-

bling, and her face was a sickly white. "Sooner or later, that thing'll kill my son unless . . . unless it's stopped somehow."

"Can't we do anything?"

"What's to be done?" replied Hester with a kind of sob. "If we was to go to Luther's aid, it'd only put three people in danger instead of just one. There's no book of rules I know of on how to handle a buzz saw that's taken on a life of its own. It appears to be immortal, so long as that polish covers it."

"Even the hardest scrubbing won't take off the polish," moaned Dorcas. "That stuff sticks worse'n any glue ever made."

The woman and the girl looked at one another. There were tears in the eyes of each. Then, all at once, Dorcas's eyes widened.

"We can do it," she said, almost to herself. "At least we've got to try."

"Do what, girl?" asked Hester.

"No time for explanations," Dorcas snapped. "Just follow my lead."

Dorcas looked about until she spied Mayor Phipps's bald head.

"Mayor," she called, "I want you to go back into town. When you get there, you're to—"

A loud shriek of the saw drowned out the rest of Dorcas's orders from Hester's hearing.

"See here, Dorcas Taney," sputtered the mayor. "Who are you to be giving commands to me? I'll have you know—"

"Mayor Phipps!" said Hester in a steely voice. "That's my son in the clearing with the saw. If Dorcas thinks she knows some way to save him, you do as she says. If not—or if any harm comes to Luther—I'm coming into town with my cast-iron skillet and bust it over your head. D'you understand me, sir?"

"Ye . . . yes, Hester. But Dorcas, it'll take a while to—"

"Just you get a move on, Mayor. Miz Gilpin, you come with me."

"Where are we off to, girl?"

"Like you said to the mayor, ma'am, I'm giving the orders now. Let's go."

Dorcas and Hester went plunging off through the woods, leaving Luther to continue his battle with the buzz saw.

WHEEEEEEEEEE

CHAPTER NINE

It's Better'n Anything

For the better part of half an hour, Luther held the buzz saw at bay in the clearing. Every time the enormous machine headed for a tree to do some more cutting, he'd fling sticks and stones at it and then run away when it charged at him.

At first, the clumsy movements of the saw table's wooden legs slowed it down, and Luther could easily avoid the spinning blade. As time passed, however, the thing seemed to learn how to move about with more agility. At each of Luther's feints and dodges, the blade missed him by a narrower margin. At one point Luther tripped, and the saw hunkered down so the bottom of the blade touched the ground.

WHEEEEEEE

The blade plowed a slot through the fallen leaves as it headed straight for the boy. It would have had him for sure if the teeth hadn't hit a stone, slowing it down and giving him time to roll aside.

Meanwhile, all us onlookers stood at the edge of the clearing, and everyone was too scared to go to the boy's aid. The way we figured, there could be only one outcome. Sooner or later Luther would tire or make a false move. Then the saw would have him.

Luther dashed across the clearing and leaned against a tree, panting for breath. Slowly the saw approached, like a hunter stalking his prey.

Just then, we all heard the clopping of horses' hoofs, pounding along the trail to the sawmill, and the squeak of wooden wheels, and the jingle of harness. A loud cheer went up as Mayor Phipps arrived, sitting high on the wooden seat and urging on a pair of matched gray horses.

He was driving the pumper wagon from the Coven Tree firehouse. Resting on the wagon bed was a great silvery tank, and from the way the horses were straining, the tank was full up with water. The giant pump was bolted to the tank's top, its huge piston attached by brass levers to two hardwood poles that ran the length of the wagon, one on each side. When ten or a dozen men grasped each of these poles and began working them up and down, water could be pumped through the hose hard enough to reach the top of the tallest building in Coven Tree. The whole apparatus looked magnificent as it glided among the trees, for the volunteer firemen always kept it in first-class condition.

"Here, you folks!" bawled the mayor. "Let's get this thing to working before something happens to Luther there!"

Nobody needed any further urging. A number of men and women grasped at the pump handles, unfolding them and locking them into position. Each of the handles was nearly fifteen feet long, and people formed lines on both sides of the wagon, flexing their arms and getting ready to pump.

At the same time, others unrolled one of the hoses. They attached one end to the pump and screwed a great brass nozzle to the other. Sven Hensen, and two other men nearly as strong, gripped the nozzle as if it were the head of an enormous snake.

"All right, now!" Mayor Phipps ordered. "Let 'er rip!"

With that, the pumpers on the wagon's right side pushed up on their pole, while those on the left pulled down. "One!" they all shouted at once.

Then they reversed their movements. "Two!"

Slowly at first, and then faster and faster the pump handles moved. Up . . . down . . . up . . . down, up, down, updownupdownupdown . . .

All at once water spewed out of the hose nozzle, soaking some folks who hadn't had the wisdom to get out of the way. "Turn it on the saw!" cried the mayor. "Knock it flat, if you can!"

The nozzle turned, and the stream of water smashed against the flat, whirring blade. For a moment the saw staggered, but it didn't go down. It turned about to face the pumper wagon.

WHEEEEEE

"Look out!" screamed one of the men at the pump. "It's coming this way!"

Everybody on the pump handles let go and scurried off among the trees. "That thing'll cut the tank right in two!" bawled a voice.

Quick as a wink, Luther stooped down and pried a pair of rocks loose from the ground. "Take that!" he shouted, flinging one of them at the saw. It bonged against the whirling blade. "And that!"

As the saw turned about to face him again, Luther's heart sank. If even the gushing water of the fire hose couldn't wash off Professor Popkin's

Prodigious Polish, what chance did he have to . . .

That's when Hester Gilpin and Dorcas Taney came staggering back through the woods toward the clearing. They both clutched the handle of a big iron pot, black and battered with use. From the way they were bent by its weight, the pot was filled near to the brim with . . . with something.

They set the pot down next to the pumper with a thump. "I sure hope your idea works, Dorcas," said Hester, wiping her brow on a sleeve of her dress. "Luther looks plumb tuckered out from fighting that saw."

"Hester Gilpin, what have you got in that pot?" the mayor demanded.

"No time to explain now, Mayor Phipps," snapped Dorcas. "You just climb up there on top of the tank and open up the filler hole."

"But . . ."

"Do as the girl says, Eli," said Hester. "Luther don't look like he can last much longer, fighting that saw."

With much puffing and groaning, Eli Phipps hauled himself up the side of the wagon until he was sitting on the tank. He unscrewed a large brass cap on its top.

"What next?" he asked.

"Pour this inside." Between them, Hester and Dorcas lifted the pot to where the mayor could reach it.

"But . . . Well, all right, if you say so."

With that, Mayor Phipps tilted the pot over the filler hole.

A thick glop, lumpy and grayish white, began pouring from the lip of the pot down into the pumper tank. The mayor continued pouring until the pot was completely upended.

"Here's a stick, Eli," said Hester. "Scrape at the pot until every last bit of that stuff comes out."

The mayor did as he was told. When he'd finished, he tossed the empty pot back onto the ground, screwed the brass cap into place, and climbed down himself.

"I got that messy stuff all over my best clothes," he said. "They're completely ruined."

"No they ain't, Mayor," said Dorcas with a wide grin. "You just soak 'em in water, and they'll come cleaner than they ever were. There ain't *nothin'* that Miz Gilpin's lye soap won't wash off. It's better'n anything. And you just poured a year's supply into the tank."

"I've not found anything yet that my soap can't

get clean," added Hester. "I just pray it'll work on that polish covering the saw."

She turned toward the clearing. "Luther? Are you all right out there?"

"For the moment, Ma," he called back. "But I'm mighty tired, and that's a fact."

"Then let's have everybody at their stations again," Hester commanded. "Get to pumping. Wet down that saw as if you were trying to drown it."

The pumpers returned to their places, and Sven and his helpers gripped the nozzle. Up . . . down . . . up, down, updownupdown . . .

Again water gushed forth. But this time, mixed with the soap, it foamed like waves breaking on the seashore. The nozzle turned toward the saw and the spurting foam smashed against the blade.

WHEEEEEEEE

The saw howled angrily. It spun about to face the pumper.

"Keep going, everybody!" yelled Dorcas. "It's the only chance we got!"

WHEEEE

"I think it's weakening!" called Luther. "Try and spray the other side."

The men at the hose moved across the clearing

and shot another stream of water at the saw's far side.

WHEE

The spinning blade slowed.

WHEE . . . WHAAaaaa . . . ooohh . . .

It stopped.

"Keep at it. Keep spraying." Mayor Phipps danced about like a man possessed. "We're winning."

Yet another gush of foamy water struck the wide blade. The saw toppled to its side like a felled tree and lay still amid the duff of the forest floor.

Warily the crowd approached it. "Careful there," said Hester. "It may still be—"

Slowly the blade spun half around as if exhausted from the day's activity.

"Now get some rags," Hester went on. "Soak 'em good from the hose and wash every speck of that polish off. Don't miss a single spot. Dorcas, where'd you go to, girl?"

Hester looked about. Over near the sawmill, Luther was lying on the ground, weak from his ordeal and gasping for air. Dorcas sat with his head in her lap, stroking his hair and whispering something that just the two of them could hear.

"We'll do just fine here," Hester murmured,

more to herself than to Dorcas. "I expect you and Luther have got more important things on your minds."

Stew Meat here again. I guess my tale of Professor Popkin's Prodigious Polish is nearing its end.

After the saw'd been scrubbed down and set back into place, there was still plenty of soapy water in the pumper tank. We used it to scrub off the school bell and the Quists' ax and all those other things that'd been polished. So, once more, our village of Coven Tree got back to something resembling normal living.

Luther? He had to work hard on the Gilpin farm for several months to earn the money he owed me for replacing the stove at the Quists', and for the Widow Vedder's new plow and the doll he'd promised Ruby Lecky. During that time, he decided farming was a lot more pleasurable—and peaceful—than traveling the land and trying to sell stuff to strangers.

Oh, now and again he gets to dreaming of what might have been and wondering if, perhaps, there might be a market for his ma's lye soap. But Dorcas Taney has a way of talking him out of such tomfoolery.

He packed up that crate of bottles and sent 'em all back to that place in Netherton. You remember—the town that never was. Even though Luther put his own return address up in the corner of the crate, it never came back to him. So it must have ended up . . . someplace.

So if any of you come across that crate of bottles, my best advice is to leave it be. But if, perhaps, curiosity gets the best of you—and if a strange smiling man comes by in the dark of night—here's something to keep in mind:

Luther's ma, Hester Gilpin, knows how to make the best soap that ever was. And she'd be more than happy to sell you a can or two, if ever you have a need for it.

About the Author

Bill Brittain's tales of the rural New England village of Coven Tree are well-loved by children of all ages. *The Wish Giver* was a 1984 Newbery Honor Book; it and *Devil's Donkey* were both named ALA Notable Children's Books as well as *School Library Journal* Best Books. A third Coven Tree novel, *Dr. Dredd's Wagon of Wonders*, was a 1988 Children's Editors' Choice (ALA *Booklist*).

Mr. Brittain has also written many other delightful books for Harper & Row, including *All the Money in the World*, which won the 1982–1983 Charlie May Simon Children's Book Award and was adapted for television as an ABC–TV Saturday Special. His fast-paced mystery *Who Knew There'd Be Ghosts?* was a Children's Choice for 1986 (IRA/CBC), while *The Fantastic Freshman* was named a Children's Choice for 1989 and an ALA Recommended Book for Reluctant Young Adult Readers. Most recently, he wrote the delightful comedy thriller *My Buddy, the King*, a 1990 Children's Choice Book (IRA/CBC).

The author of over 65 mystery stories, which have appeared in *Ellery Queen's Mystery Magazine*, *Alfred Hitchcock's Mystery Magazine*, and several other anthologies, Bill Brittain lives with his wife, Ginny, in Asheville, North Carolina.

About the Artist

Andrew Glass is a well-known illustrator of fantasy and adventure stories for young readers. He has illustrated all of Bill Brittain's Coven Tree tales, and in addition, he has illustrated *Banjo*, by Robert Newton Peck; *Spooky Night*, by Natalie Savage Carlson; and the 1983 Newbery Honor Book *Graven Images* by Paul Fleishman. Mr. Glass is also the author and illustrator of three picture books: *Jackson Makes His Move*, *My Brother Tries to Make Me Laugh* and *Chick Pea and the Talking Cow*. He lives and works in New York City.